"*M in the Middle* provides one of the best insights that I have ever read into the world not only of teenage girls but of all people on the spectrum, and does so while still being entertaining, well written, funny and moving. Beyond its obvious readership, it should be required reading for all neurotypical teenagers with the purpose of developing empathy for the struggles their peers on the spectrum face, particularly in mainstream education. I will be recommending it to everyone, everywhere."

– *Davida Hartman, Director and Senior Educational Psychologist at The Children's Clinic, Dublin and author of* The Growing Up Guide for Girls: What Girls on the Autism Spectrum Need to Know!

"Really nice to hear more about M. She has a brilliant way of describing autism, in particular the sensory experiences and the desire to belong and be "normal," whilst being aware of her anxiety and her limits. I could relate very much to her need to know why, her need for exact timings and structure, and her confusion about why people don't say exactly what they mean. This book will help a lot of young girls feel a lot less alone."

– *Alis Rowe, Entrepreneur and Founder of the Curly Hair Project*

"I wanted to wrap my arms around M – and her story – and never let go. This glimpse of the world through her eyes is touching, taut and – most importantly – truthful."

– *Karen McCombie, author of* The Whispers of Wilderwood Hall, The OMG Blog *and many more*

"An insightful and honest page turner with a distinctive voice and a wonderfully engaging heroine. A truly remarkable achievement by Vicky Martin and the students of Limpsfield Grange."

– *Katy Birchall, author of* The It Girl *series*

M in the Middle

by the same authors

M is for Autism
*The Students of Limpsfield
Grange School and Vicky Martin*
ISBN 978 1 78592 034 9
eISBN 978 1 78450 286 7

in the middle

Secret Crushes, Mega-Colossal Anxiety and the People's Republic of Autism

The Students of
Limpsfield Grange School
and Vicky Martin

Jessica Kingsley *Publishers*
London and Philadelphia

First published in 2017
by Jessica Kingsley Publishers
73 Collier Street
London N1 9BE, UK
and
400 Market Street, Suite 400
Philadelphia, PA 19106, USA

www.jkp.com

Library of Congress Cataloging in Publication Data
A CIP catalog record for this book is available from
the Library of Congress

British Library Cataloguing in Publication Data
A CIP catalogue record for this book is available from the British Library

ISBN 978 1 78592 034 9
eISBN 978 1 78450 286 7

Printed and bound in Great Britain

MIX
Paper from
responsible sources
FSC® C013056

Thank you to Sarah Wild and all the staff and families at Limpsfield Grange for their time, support and expertise.

Part 1

M'S World

Secretly, I just want to be normal.

★ Chapter 1 ★

FROM: J.Twinnings@st.andrews.ac.uk

TO: ALL STAFF

**Subject: Year 8 Student –
AUTISM DIAGNOSIS**

Dear all,

Please be aware that I received a copy of letter from local NHS Trust that student M has a diagnosis of autism. Her mother requested that I make staff all aware of this.

Any problems, I am available 1–2pm Tuesdays to Thursdays.

Regards,

Jill

Head of Pastoral Care

The Head of Pastoral Care, Miss Twinnings, sent an email to all the staff, explaining that I had a diagnosis of autism. Mum had to chase it up a few times but on November 30th she finally sent it. I heard Mum on the phone to her friend Jackie.

"Seriously, Jacks, this bloody Head of Pastoral Care woman is so unhelpful... I just don't think she believed that M has autism... I had to practically send the email myself!"

Year 8 started well. It was much better than Year 7. Which had been difficult with Nev and Lara and their stirring and causing trouble for me and my anxiety had got really bad, out of control, but after I got the diagnosis things in my life began to make more sense. Me and Mum realised I wasn't going mad and I wasn't weird, it's just I experienced the world differently.

My diagnosis gave me some stability... So when I went into Year 8 I felt like I knew myself a bit more. As Fiona my counsellor said,

"Life is going in the right direction and this is really positive."

And just like what Mum's fridge magnet says,

POSITIVE THINGS HAPPEN TO POSITIVE PEOPLE!

I was able to concentrate more on my school work. I found new ways of working and even new ways of walking around the school, which made me much happier. Much more relaxed.

But stability can W-O-ʙ-B-L-e. Stability is a state that gets challenged and battered all the time. I like stability. I want stability but I wobble a lot.

Lots of the teachers were more understanding to me after the email, but some teachers, like Mrs Chiswick, who teaches maths, said,

"Autism sounds like a great excuse for behaving badly and not trying hard enough."

I'm good with numbers and generally can get the answers straight away but Mrs Chiswick wants us to,

"Display our workings out in our books, otherwise I won't know if you've cheated."

Mum would look at my work and say,

"You've got a good instinct for maths M."

And I knew what she meant. I understand the numbers and where they fit well and how they should but it doesn't matter, I still get Ds because I can't explain how I get my answers.

Corridors at St. Andrew's have always been very difficult for me and most teachers let me walk around the school the way I wanted, but some teachers like

Mrs Chiswick would insist I walk along the maths corridor and wouldn't let me enter the class room via the outside fire exit. She said,

"Use the corridors efficiently, like any normal human being."

NORMAL HUMAN BEING

But you see corridors are a hostile territory to me and I wish I could saunter along them, so that I too could be one of these NORMAL HUMAN BEINGS.

Corridors echo.

Posters on the walls, s
l
i
d
e and fall.

Windows can be open or closed.

Lights flicker.

Corridors: Tunnels, lined with doors which people can exit from, **suddenly!**

Corridors off corridors. Corridors with staircases. Glass corridors. Cold blue corridors linked to overheated corridors, linked to dark brown corridors with draughts.

And corridors change frequently. Lots of people – then empty. Posters change. Noticeboards change their information. Doors open and sometimes they **SLAM** shut, rattling the glass that rattles, and lacerates my brain.

People rush down corridors.

People dawdle.

Some people d-r-a-a-a-ag their hands along corridor walls and then PULL a poster off a notice board.

Very UNPREDICTABLE PLACES!

The Beast of Anxiety lurks behind lockers and pounces on my back or waits for me, sneakily behind a door, ready to ambush me and stop me from getting to where I need to be!

And corridors mean a change of situation. Crossing into a new territory! Transitions! CHANGES! And changes are not a good thing for me.

And the blue, maths corridor is cold. And I feel like I am entering a hostile territory: unnerving peeling paint, cutting draughts and rattling windows.

RATTLING WINDOWS + DRAUGHTS = FEAR

BATTLE + RATTLE = ANXIETY

PEELING PAINT + HARSH SUNLIGHT = HEADACHE

FEAR + ANXIETY + HEADACHE

does *not* equal a good maths lesson.

So my grades in maths began to s
l
i
d
e from Cs
to Ds and Mrs Chiswick would get angry at me and slam books down on my desk and ask questions like,

"What time did you go to bed last night?"

And Joe would whisper,

"She thinks you're tired and that's why your grades are getting worse."

"Well? What time did you go to bed last night?" And I can't answer. I don't know why she is asking me this. I don't understand, and anxiety has me in a head lock and it's tightening its grip around my little neck and I am struggling to breathe. And I use all my strength, all my focus, to draw my shaky breath, deep into my lungs, like how Fiona, my counsellor, taught me. Deep, deep steadying breaths.

Deep breath in.

And out.

Deep breath in.

And out.

The truth is I went to bed last night at 9.00pm but I didn't sleep till 6.00am. I often have nights without much sleep. Mum calls them my "all-nighters." When my worries are the size of Kilimanjaro or Mars or the Great Wall of China and these are great, big enormous things that I just can't push aside at 4.00am. They sit, big, bulging in my head.

Lara's phone beeps.

Mrs Chiswick swings around and I swear she shouts at her almost with delight and stands over her desk. The attention is taken away from me and anxiety loosens its hold, a little. Joe whispers,

"She's power mad M, don't worry. I'll help you with your homework. I could come over this evening?"

So Joe likes to come over and visit and we'd do our maths homework at the kitchen table. Mum really likes him. She says,

"I like Joe, he's a very mature boy," and Toby says,

"He's cool."

Not that Toby sees him much because Toby goes out a lot. But when Joe is over he lingers at the door. Half in, half out. Very disconcerting. Toby changes when Joe is about. He acts a bit like a dad or a teacher and even called him "mate." He actually behaves like a nice person, maybe that's how he wins all the "Most Polite Boy" certificates, stuck all over the fridge. The certificates I want to rip up and throw in the bin because I don't get certificates...just letters home about my behaviour.

Dear Parent,

Your daughter's disruptive behaviour in lesson 4 on Thursday 16th October has resulted in:

A Stage 2 on St. Andrew's Code of Conduct

According to the school contract, which you signed when your child joined St. Andrew's, this means a meeting is required with head of form and Head of Pastoral Care to discuss personal and academic goals. Please attend a meeting on 17th November 8.40am.

There are lots of these letters stuffed in drawers and bags...they don't make it to the fridge door.

Anyway, Joe. Everyone really likes Joe. (Except Nev and Lara, but they don't like many people.) He's just one of those "even people" that everyone gets along with. Bella, our big, fat Labrador, likes Joe. She wags her tail and gets all excited when he comes over and Joe even takes Bella round the block if he stays for dinner and Mum always insists that he stays for dinner. She says,

"Joe, you've saved me a fortune in maths tuition." To be honest Joe does lighten the feel of the house sometimes.

"You've got a great family," said Joe one evening, while I was trying to work out the ratio of women to men in a fictitious software business in Nevada, USA.

"Really Joe? Are you serious?" I ask. "There's a bit missing," I said and Joe looked at my calculations.

"No, from my family," I reply and he laughs. He does this a lot and I used to get annoyed with him and hurt, then he explained sometimes we have "funny misunderstandings."

"Is this a funny misunderstanding, Joe?" I ask.

"Yes," he says, smiling. "Your hair looks good M."

"Thank you. I know," I say and he smiles. "I look pretty today, don't I?" And he laughs.

I know I am pretty. Everyone tells me this and I do assess from looking at pictures of other teenage girls that I'm on the high end of the pretty scale. Plus I wear really fashionable clothes and I've read things on the web and magazines that style and fashion can really enhance your attractiveness.

He flicks a pea, left over from dinner, and it hits my white school shirt.

I am shocked!

"I'm sorry M! I was only teasing."

Teasing is one of those words, concepts that I really don't understand. I've known people to tease me and it's horrible and they've got in trouble, and when Dad lived at home he would tease Toby and they'd both laugh and then I heard someone on TV saying they would "tease the information out of the suspect." So it's at points like this I have to withdraw. It's words like this which keep me separate and feeling dislocated from this world.

However, I am annoyed. He's got dinner on my white shirt.

"And what do you mean, a bit's missing from your family?" he asks.

"Well, Dad. He's not here." I don't tell him that I did it. I broke the family because my anxiety drove

Dad away and my guilt, the size of Russia, the biggest country in the world, 17,075,200 square kilometres, hangs around me all the time.

"Yeah but he's still your dad. To be honest, M," he continues, "my dad *is* around and I wish he wasn't."

"We're a broken family Joe. That's what we are called."

"I don't think it's that simple M…" And I think to myself that nothing ever, ever is that simple. How I long for simple.

"Anyway, bent, broken or cracked I really like it round yours. You get some peace."

"Peace? Really? Toby is so loud and booming and Mum is always shouting up the stairs or her phone is going off, she's listening to the TV *and* talking."

"Well, it's peaceful now," he said, and we stopped and listened. I could hear:

1. Fridge whirring intensely.

2. The kitchen light buzzing, drilling.

3. High sounding, tinny screeching coming from Mum's radio upstairs.

4. Bella's breathing.

5. Toby slamming the front door shut and shaking the whole house.

6. The neighbours plugging things in.

7. A car passing outside.

8. A car door slamming.

"This isn't peaceful, Joe."

"I've got six brothers and sisters, M. This is peaceful compared to mine." I make a mental note, *never, ever* visit Joe's.

"And your mum's really nice. She actually talks to me." And I think Mum talks too much. "My mum just shouts a lot and your mum's got a cool job." Mum is a textile designer and she makes all these amazing materials and designs, which is where everyone says I get my love of textures and colours from… But I'm not sure it works that way. Where do I get my anxiety from? Who gave me that?

Joe tidies his books away and asks if I want to go to a film on Saturday, but I can't because Dad is coming to visit on Saturday, but I'm glad I can't go because the truth is cinemas are very difficult places for me. I wait for films to come out on Netflix or the internet and anyway I need to watch some Skylar on YouTube.

Mum comes into the kitchen after Joe leaves and points to the stain on my white shirt.

"What's that?" I go to the sink and scrub at the stain.

"Joe flicked a pea at me." Mum's eyes go big and wide and she sidles across the kitchen floor to me.

"OHHHHH, somebody likes you, M," she says. "He'd be a perfect son-in-law, M! He's so polite!"

"Mum, are you suggesting that I *marry* Joe?"

"Oh, M! You could wear white and I've always thought Rose Vale House would be a perfect wedding venue!

"Are you teasing me?" I ask. A car passes on the road outside and the neighbours shut their front door, they walk up the front path, click-click – click-click on the concrete and in my head. I tap my face with my fingers and I sense The Beast of Anxiety in the room. Its eyes **lock** on me. Mum says she's sorry and she explains that she wasn't teasing me, she was dreaming of a happy future for me. I tap more.

"A future? When in the future? What time Mum? When?!!!" She's planning events, and a wedding at Rose Vale House is unfolding in front of me at a very high speed. The future is a frightening place.

"Stop it, M, please!" And I tap more and I walk towards the stairs.

"Stop what? Mum, exactly what should I stop? What have I done?" The Beast of Anxiety, eyes still locked on me, paces around the room.

"Stop getting stressed out. Please. I was just thinking about the future, when you're grown up… I was dreaming, M. It's just what mums do! Dream. I shouldn't have said anything…"

"I need to change my shirt, the smell of the pea is making me nauseous."

"It's just you seemed really on track M, in life. I was just joking around. I thought maybe I could. Did I push it too far M? I did, I pushed it too far, didn't I?"

"Shouldn't you be in love with the person you marry?" I ask.

"Yes, darling, most definitely," she answers.

"I don't love Joe."

"Well, that's very sensible of you, M, and I was just being silly."

I escape up the stairs to the safety of my little pink room and avoid a full-on assault from anxiety. I was spared this evening but I know it's still hanging around, waiting for its next opportunity. Ever present. I get into bed and wrap myself tightly in the purple and grey blanket my mum made me and I think about how I love Lynx. I should marry Lynx...

I'm supposed to be in a pack
but I haven't found it yet.

★ Chapter 2 ★

Friend

[noun]

A person you like a lot. Not usually a member of your family.

She's my best/oldest/closest friend – we've known each other since we were five.

He's a family friend/friend of the family.

My friend enquired how my holiday was.

Shaznia has been my friend at school and out of school too. We'd met up over the holidays and some Saturdays too.

And this is not easy for me.

I have to plan and need notice to prepare myself and to choose my clothes, organise my travel arrangements, and when these are in place I can meet my best friend! Yay! (I'm not sure she's actually a *best* friend. I would like that but...)

We've been over to each other's houses too. Shaznia lives at 67 Bluecoat Lane, Sevenoaks, Kent and it's not easy for me to go there but I make the effort to visit her home, with smells, colours and shapes very different to mine. And of course Anxiety always comes along too. Dragging out of me... And I try to shake it off or prise out its claws that dig and cut into me and I *try* to ignore it because you see, when you have a friend, you do things to keep the friendship going. You have to make an effort and nurture it, as it explains in the feature "How To Tell If She's A Real Friend," *Cherry Magazine*, The Friendship Special.

Sometimes your friend will want to go swimming and sometimes you'll want to go drink caramel café lattes at the local coffee shop! But remember, make the effort to do things she loves too! Nurture that friendship and watch it blossom!

I never talk about having autism with Shaznia. I'm not ashamed of it...but sometimes I am... Often her aunt is in her kitchen and says things like, "Is she the little one with the criminal's disease?" Shaznia and her mum tell her to be quiet and of course I don't have a criminal disease, I know this. But sometimes I catch a flicker, a flash, a change cross Shaznia's face and I worry that it's doubt or fear about our friendship, so I try to make small talk to make her feel better. I say,

"Shaznia, I'm enquiring about your holiday and how it was?" Like it says in the dictionary, and her aunt will see I am a good friend, not a criminal.

But her aunt **BANGED** the table and laughed and her mum says,

"M, that's very sweet of you to ask. Our last holiday was in the Lake District and we had a very enjoyable time. You girls go upstairs and I'll bring you some lemonade."

I don't like Shaznia's aunt one bit but I don't say anything to my mum in case she stops me seeing Shaznia. However, I try not to go to her house that much or I ask if she'll be there and Shaznia says "yes" and "sorry" and that she feels bad about her aunt. It's nice that Shaznia cares. Also, we have "lots in common." Another definition in "How To Tell If She's A Real Friend." We both love clothes! We love trying on combinations of shoes, skirts, jewellery, socks, bags, etc... She really listens to my advice about what to wear and how to apply make-up and I really like this. It makes me feel really good about myself.

I understand colours and textures and shapes much more than other girls my age do and I can match shoes and nail polish and all the little details that really bring an outfit to life!

I also copy Skylar, The All-American Girl. Pop star and icon for the 21st century. She always looks so beautiful and is so popular and often has an American twist to some of her outfits like the Star Spangled Banner skirt she wore in season 7, episode 15 in which she visits the American President and discovers that the White House domestic supervisor (we would call him a cleaner) is a spy for another presidential candidate, Newton Layburn Senior. Skylar uncovers this "threat to democracy" and ends up performing on the 5th of July, in Capitol Hill, and the American President closes the episode saying,

"You really are our all-American girl Skylar!" And she cries and looks up at a shooting star travelling across the night sky. I probably wouldn't wear that outfit, unless it was for fancy dress, but usually I copy the clothes she wears when relaxing on the tour bus or visiting children's hospices in Oklahoma or Florida.

Another thing me and Shaznia have in common is we like to talk about LOVE.

Love – the most exciting, joyous, beautiful part of my life!

When Shaznia talks about boys and love, I have to sit on my hands or hold them tightly and breathe deeply, so I don't flap or tap my face and I am elated that she talks to *me* about these things. In fact I can hardly believe it. I'm like one of those girls in *Cherry Magazine*, sitting in a coffee shop, laughing with their friends. Shaznia must think I am cool enough, and that acceptance gives me joy much bigger than the world! Shaznia does talk a lot. Mum asked if she talks "too much," but I love it because I don't have to do "small talk," which inevitably causes me a lot of problems. It is excruciating and pointless. Toby calls Shaznia The Gob. Mum laughs but then stops and says,

"Stop it Toby. That's not nice."

I sit on the edge of her bed, as the bean bag is very strange and Shaznia's bedroom is so cool. She has a double wardrobe and we go through each item assessing if it suits her or what she can combine it with to create a successful outfit. And I love that her mum brings us lemonade and cake and says,

"Shaznia isn't going on about her clothes too much, is she M?"

And I look at her silver and pink clock and watch the hands go round and round, amazed at how much time can have passed, and I feel so included and part of real teen life. But the best bit is when we talk about boys and how much we love Lynx and Jake. Lynx and Jake are in Year 10 and are best friends. They are always with each other, which, as Shaznia says, would be perfect for a double date!

And we plan trips up town to see if we can meet them and then *pretend* it's an accident. I don't understand why we would pretend it's an accident but I don't want to disturb our friendship in any way. When Mum collects me in the car she always asks,

"Does Shaznia *ever* ask you any questions?"

And I say,

"Yes, she asked me if her sky blue top and grey leggings matched."

"But does she ask any questions about YOU, M?" And I go a bit quiet because she doesn't but I really like it that way, and Mum tightens her lips and shakes her head and I say,

"What are you doing Mum? What does that mean?"

"I just think you could do better than Shaznia as a friend."

"Are you disapproving of my friendship?" I ask, and she shrugs her shoulders and says,

"Why don't you spend more time with Joe? He's a good friend."

But I think Mum just doesn't understand. We are friends. It may not be a friendship like her and Jackie, who drink white wine all the time and sing along to old songs and then start crying, but it's the kind of friendship I want…although it is…tiring but I won't tell anyone that. I put on my friendship mask and I am a friend! A good friend! I can do it!

For my birthday last year Shaznia bought me the kind of card I'd always dreamed of receiving. It was a big card – 20 cm × 30 cm – and had a pink, sparkly tassel in the middle. On the cover it had a teddy bear dressed in a prom dress, wearing high, silver heels and wearing lots of diamonds and she / it was holding a heart-shaped handbag. She / It was climbing into a pearl coloured limousine and inside the card it had a poem printed in pink:

Friendships are precious!
Friendships are special!

Which makes you special and precious to me!
Happy birthday Style Queen

And wrapped in pink heart paper was a bottle of Skylar, Jet Set perfume. (Toby said it smelt like the day the drains burst on our street – it didn't.) And I've placed it on a shelf in my room, with the card, one of Dad's guitar plectrums, a photograph of my grandad who died and a Buddha Mum gave me. And they are all on that shelf because they are important to me.

And also, if I hang out with Shaznia, there is more chance I will get to see Lynx, the juicy-lipped, hair-gelled love of my life.

LYNX

The first time I saw Lynx I was struck by love.
STRUCK. It's the day I realised how I
am merely a vessel for all these emotions and
how they lie dormant in my body and I lug
them around all the time and then they burst
or crash or slide or burn or smash out of me.

My love for Lynx is like Skylar's love for
Ewan. She loves him because she feels
"connected" to him. That's how I feel about
Lynx! Connected... But Skylar and Ewan can't
be together because they both have to play
concerts with their really cool bands and tour
different parts of America and the world! In
season 5, episode 4 she says,

"Ewan, I love you, to the moon and back, but,
baby, I need to sing. The world needs to hear
my voice and I just can't see how I can commit
to a full-time relationship."

And then he fights back tears and says,

"I'll wait."

He hands her a gold heart necklace and says,

"When you look up to the night sky and see a shooting star, think of me and know that I am always here for you Skylar. We are connected. Souls connected for ever."

And then he walks up the steps to a private jet because he is in a band too and is playing Chicago that night.

Sometimes at the end of an episode she falls asleep, on a hotel bed, crying tears of love (Tears of Love is also the name of her album), gripping the gold heart, and then a shooting star crashes across the sky to where Ewan is in Mexico or San Francisco or Ontario and he looks up at the star and knows...he knows that Skylar is thinking about him...but they can't be together right now...but she really,

really loves him. And I think it's the same way that I feel. Stars crashing, Love as big and epic as a night sky!

I am sure he is my Ewan. I've never actually spoken to Lynx.

My anxiety is like an alarm
that never, ever stops.

★ Chapter 3 ★

Joe is sitting next to me in break, telling me about the player formation in the football last night, which is very interesting. Toby had been watching it before he went to the cinema but the crowd's relentless chanting, chanting, chanting and roars meant I had to go to my room, and the likely event of Toby shouting out unexpectedly meant I had to retreat. When he does this I feel like anxiety is booting me in the chest and I can't breathe. So I took myself away from potential harm.

Corridors, noises and difficult instructions always cause me distress at school but I had been doing very well that day, that week. I was *managing*. Shaznia came up to me at form time and asked if I wanted to go to town. She had some vouchers and wanted my advice on some new trainers but I couldn't go.

Her face dropped and she let out a sigh. Was she hurt? I didn't mean to upset her.

"What are you doing instead?" she asked.

"I have to see my dad this weekend."

"Cancel!" she said. A wave of nausea swept through me and I sense The Beast of Anxiety watching me from the doorway. Just skulking and waiting for an opportunity to attack me.

"Oh go on. Come with me M! Cancel. I've got some vouchers for Coffee Star too. We can sit by the fountain. You like the fountain, don't you?" It's true I quite like the fountain and the rushing water. A little bit of nature amongst all the concrete and neon lights.

My mouth goes dry and I feel a ton of pressure weigh down on me.

"Sorry, I just can't." Her voice got louder and my body tightened. Anxiety, snarling, edges closer to me.

"You could come over to mine after?" She pauses. "My aunt won't be there."

"I can't Shaznia." (How many times do I have to tell her?)

"Oh that's a shame. Are you sure? Could you go to your dad's on *Sunday*?" she suggested. I tapped my face.

SHAME AND LIES

SHAME AND LIES

"But she's planned to go to her dad's on *Saturday*."

Shaznia ignores Joe and continued,

"Jake told Dawn, in Year 9, who gets the bus with me on Monday, that he was going to Sports Rite on Saturday morning, so that means Lynx and Jake will be in town, because they are always together and I can wear that pink checked skirt and we could do our nails. You could do my nails with that sunset gel varnish."

Bus. Sports Rite. Town. LYNX. Sunset nail gel varnish. I want it all. My heart sank. Low. But it's just not possible.

"I can't Shaznia."

She tuts and says,

"I'll ask someone else then."

And she sat on Nev's desk and asked if she wanted to go instead.

"Oh how quick we are replaced!" says Joe.

Is she really replacing me? Will she still be my friend? I place my hands on the desk and take a deep breath because she's just thrown town at me and all its noises and smells and lights and I'm just not prepared. I'm not.

Anxiety hangs about the class room... Its cruel, heavy eyes watching my every move. Judging. Sneering. Intimidating me.

And I've told a lie. A nasty lie that is sitting in my guts and eating away at me. The LIE which is sitting in my stomach like a coiled tape worm. I've seen pictures of them in science, all coiled up in jars, removed from Victorian women's stomachs, who used to eat them to lose weight.

"I didn't think you were going to visit your dad's again," says Joe. And he's right, and now he knows I am a liar too.

OVAL OVAL OVAL

The Oval is a hole I've fallen into many, many times. It's Nan's home. My dad's mum and now Dad lives there too. He grew up there but left when he met Mum. But when they separated he moved back to The Oval and took all his guitars and records with him.

Days before our twice-monthly visit I would be teetering on the edge of the Oval hole. Wobbling until finally I would be thrown into the Oval abyss and by *my parents*. Thrown in by the people who are meant to look after me! Protect me from danger.

Visits to The Oval were a grey overload with sharp, concrete edges with 48 cold, grey steps and at the top of the 48 grey steps is my nan's flat. Damp and stinking of overcooked cabbage, whiskey and cigarettes and The Oval has orange slices too. Orange wallpaper and orange curtains, and two particularly harsh, lime green scratchy cushions and nicotine net curtains that hang at her super, shiny, clean windows.

My nerves ripped and I'd cry and scream and Nan wouldn't say, "What's wrong with her?" She'd suck on her cigarette and say,

"You've got problems lined up with that little one."

One visit I was lining up the switches and knobs on her cooker and one came off in my little hand and she immediately **smacked** me across the back of my little chubby legs.

"You naughty, naughty little girl," she yelled in my face, and it was an accident but I couldn't tell her that, and then she spoke as if I wasn't in the room.

"Amanda, you've got big trouble ahead with her unless you stick in a bit of good old-fashioned discipline." Mum rushed over to me and rubbed my leg and that made it worse! Her touching and rubbing their stains into my skin. "I don't care what anyone says, there is nothing wrong with raising your hand to a naughty child." And I had never been smacked before, and the shock and the pain rushed into me and I shook with fear and Nan kept talking. "Some kids need a smack. Children need to know who is in charge, Amanda, who is the boss." And Mum said,

"Don't ever touch my daughter again."

And Nan replied,

"Get her to behave and respect my property and I won't have to."

And on every visit to The Oval I would scream the whole way and struggle and contort myself to escape from my car seat. Mum and Dad would argue the whole way and Toby had his head phones on, looking out the window. Detached from all the stress and the family. My anxiety and screams would rise as we got nearer and nearer The Oval.

Dartford.

Bexley.

Isle of Dogs.

Sidcup – and at Sidcup they always started the same argument.

"It's just twice a month," Dad would say. "We see your bloody mother all the time."

"M can't cope. Look at her." And she'd turn and rub my shaking legs and she'd say,

"It's OK, baby, it's OK."

But it wasn't OK. That was the problem. I may have only been a very little girl but I knew we were heading towards The Oval and Nan's flat at the top of the grey stairwell.

"The problem is, you're a snob," he'd say to my mum.

"What's that got to do with anything? I am not a snob."

"You don't like going to my mother's because she lives in a council flat and now that's rubbing off on our daughter and that's why she kicks up this fuss every time."

FUSS FUSS FUSS

Fuss is a word that gets used a lot towards me. I seem to have spent a life time causing a FUSS.

I've since looked fuss up in the dictionary and this is what it says:

Fuss

[noun]

1. An excessive display of anxious attention or activity; needless or useless bustle: They made a fuss over the new baby.

2. A complaint or protest, especially about something relatively unimportant.

[verb]

1. To make a fuss; make much ado about trifles.

Am I relatively unimportant?

Trifles?

"She has to learn to travel in a car and come in to London and see her family. She is just a child and we have to guide her," my dad would state as I tried to squirm out of the seatbelt, which would be pressing into my little bones.

"Even if she doesn't like it?" Mum would argue.

"Yes! I had to go on visits when I was a child. It's training for life. Look at Toby. He's not making a fuss."

FUSS FUSS FUSS

"But Simon, she's so distressed. Look at her!" And I'd see his eyes dart to me in his rear view mirror and I could see his eyes soften.

"I know... I know... Look, I guess it's just a phase. Aren't we doing the right thing taking her to see her nan? Isn't this what normal families do on a Sunday? I'm just trying here!"

"I know... I know..." Mum would half agree, "but I'm not a snob, Simon."

And then we'd stand at the bottom of the stairwell and I knew that terrible fate awaited me. It doesn't get better. I never get *used* to things. Doing stressful things often and more doesn't make it easier. I just know what's going to happen, i.e. Anxiety will launch a full-blown assault on my little body. Entering the harsh world of my sharp orange nan never changed. I would envy Toby, as he stomped up the stairs with his ear phones still on and I'd stand by the first, cold, hard step listening to Mum and Dad's usual argument.

"Maybe she had a bad experience on the stairs that we don't know about," my mum would say. "Maybe when your mum took her out."

"Don't blame my mum."

"Maybe she met a nasty dog on the landing and it's given her a scare and your mother never told us." Dad would mumble at this theory and walk up the steps ahead of us.

But it wasn't a nasty dog, it was anxiety attacking, and it was the dread and fear of being trapped in a flat with overwhelming smells and tensions. And The Beast shows no mercy to age – even as a little girl it would pull and jostle me about the stairwells and throw me, terrified, near the edge of the concrete steps, as I screamed inside, gasping for breath and for someone to understand! To believe me!

Mum would try and coax me up the stairs and sometimes she just lifted me screaming, saying,

"Sorry, sorry, sweet heart. We won't stay long."

But it always felt like a very, very long time when we visited The Oval, and the last three times we visited I would not get out of the car and I ate my dinner sitting in the back seat, in the car park. Mum and Nan agreed it wasn't working and I stopped my visits.

So the truth is I wasn't going to The Oval at the weekend. I don't go to The Oval any more. I lied, a nasty, dirty lie eroding me.

Talking about my feelings helps
me clear my head...so I can deal
with a few more days...

⋆ Chapter 4 ⋆

❦ TUESDAY 4.00PM

The day I told the lie about going to visit Dad was a Tuesday. I wasn't pleased that I had told a lie – at all – but I was pleased that I told the lie on a Tuesday, as it meant maybe I could sort it all out, with Fiona. I see Fiona every Tuesday at 4.00. The powder blue room with beige chairs and a picture of three pebbles by a calm lake and the word Tranquillity underneath. Every Tuesday I leave school at 3.30. Walk, quickly, to the Good Life Therapy and Counselling Centre.

Good Life
Therapy Centre

A place to thrive and
reach your full potential

Fiona Lacy, PhD, LLC
Child & Adolescent Psychological Services

And this is why I go every Tuesday because I want a good life and I do want to thrive and reach my full potential. I don't want a life of standing in cold stairwells or lying to people, but I make sure no one sees me as I run out of English. Fiona, my counsellor, says talking to a professional is perfectly normal and is a really positive life choice but I'm not sure Nev or Lara would agree with that...so I move fast on Tuesdays. Along the marbled, speckled corridor and I glance towards Science Room 3, where Lynx has just had Physics before he goes to football practice.

I want a **Good Life**.

Up the three steps to the school reception, slowing my pace down, to avoid Debbie, the Head's PA, who shouts,

"DON'T RUN!"

And I want to say back,

"Don't shout!"

Past the Head's office. The Head.

HEAD HEAD HEAD HEAD

Count the Roman Coins in the glass cabinets – 12.

Down to the cloak room. Through the staff car park and exit the clanging school gates.

Along Vale Drive to a **Good Life**.

I like to arrive 10 minutes early and sit in the waiting room and I think about what I will say to Fiona and how I can work towards a **Good Life**! Sometimes the school gates are repeatedly clanging shut in my head or Debbie's "DON'T RUN!" bats about inside my skull, but today it's the tape worm LIE I told Shaznia which I've brought with me. LIAR.

The lie **twitches** and **wriggles** in my tummy and it feels like it might wake up fully and travel all round my body and take me over, **squirm** up my throat and crawl out my mouth.

The waiting room clock ticks its way to 4.00 and then wonderfully, beautifully, soft, reassuringly honest Fiona opens the door to the safe powder blue space. At 4.00 exactly! And says,

"Hello M. Do come in."

And I love this. I LOVE this. Every week 4.00.

TICK TICK TICK

4.00 door opens.

We sit. She smiles. I copy her and smile too.

COUNSELLOR SILENCE

And she says,

"Tell me about your week M."

And even though my weeks are full of anxiety and confusion, with possible splashes of golden good times, I want to clap my hands in joy at this predictable, ordered series of events. Why, oh why can't all of life be like this?

And the lie twitches and I break the **COUNSELLOR SILENCE** and tell her about what I said. I'm wondering if I get the LIE out here maybe I could leave it in the room. I finish telling Fiona about Shaznia and what happened and trail off... I feel so guilty, I look up at the framed black and white picture of three pebbles by a lake. Tranquillity.

"Lies can be very...helpful sometimes," states Fiona. My eyes dart from the picture to her eyes – fleetingly.

"Sounds to me like you were being very wise and protecting yourself from a difficult situation. I commend you for your quick thinking M." And the LIE does leave me!

I feel it practically travel up from my tummy, through my oesophagus, throat and my mouth and past my lips as I say,

"Really?"

And the tape worm lie slithers through the gap under the door. Gone.

And Fiona continues,

"It's good in life if we can tell the truth, so that people know how we honestly feel, but sometimes that can be difficult. And M, I think you must have been put in a very difficult situation and felt you had no other option."

I nod my head.

"What could you do next time Shaznia asks you to go to town and you don't want to go?"

I truly don't know. I look at the gap under the door. Oh God don't come back tape worm! Fiona tilts her head and makes eye contact with me and draws me back to my counselling.

But I am panicked.

"Well, I have a suggestion," she continues. "Maybe next time you could say, 'No thank you Shaznia, I just don't feel like going to town this Saturday but how about the following Saturday?' That way you haven't told a lie, and remember you don't have to explain yourself to everyone, all the time."

COUNSELLOR SILENCE

I break through the silence.

"Shaznia is quite…" And as I try to find my words…

COUNSELLOR SILENCE

"...but you see, she just keeps asking me. Shaznia doesn't really give up."

COUNSELLOR SILENCE

"And she *would* ask me to explain myself. But we're friends, so I guess she just wants to know what I'm doing and that's what friends do, don't they?"

"Friends also respect boundaries and privacy," says Fiona.

"Yes, but friends share secrets good and bad. Friendships are gold, like treasure." Fiona adjusts her glasses and says,

"Tell me more about what you just said."

"Shaznia sent me a birthday card last year and in gold writing it said,

My friend, it's you I can tell
my secrets, good and bad

And I am here for you when life is sad

I think you are an angel!
Where are your wings?!

*Because you always know how
to say the right things
The joy you give me is impossible to measure
A friendship like ours is
golden, like treasure."*

BIG COUNSELLOR SILENCE

This counsellor silence feels different and her eyebrows tighten. I am wondering if Fiona is annoyed or angry and she says,

"I would like to add a final line to that M: 'Friends respect boundaries and privacy and don't pressurise us into doing things we do not want to do.'"

"But it doesn't rhyme Fiona." And she smiles.

"No, but it is very important that you remember that. We'll talk about it more next time I see you."

And our 50 minutes is up and I leave the powder blue room. As always I leave feeling much better about my life but I do hope I haven't loosened the tape worm lie to slither about in Sevenoaks. Mum is in the waiting room and we go home.

Meltdowns are not fun. It's like being stuck on a rollercoaster for eternity... in the dark with flashing lights. Everything stops making sense.

★ Chapter 5 ★

Meltdown

[noun]

1. The melting of a significant portion of a nuclear-reactor core due to inadequate cooling of the fuel elements, a condition that could lead to the escape of radiation.

2. A quickly developing breakdown or collapse.

Toby is slurping and crunching cereal, then hurls his bowl and spoon into the sink. The crashing sound blasts through my head.

"Sorry simpleton. Did that noise upset you?"

"Stop it Toby!" shouts Mum as she makes my cheese sandwich, which she wraps tightly in cling film. Bella is sniffing around, hoping she might be in with a chance of some food. I glare at Toby.

I genuinely think he can only communicate with me by insults. So I insult him back,

"Yes it does, Idiot."

And that makes him laugh. It wasn't meant to. Why can't I hurt or wind other people up as much as they do to me? Why do I always miss the target? I just want a little bit of revenge. I just want Toby to know how I feel.

He opens the fridge door and glugs orange juice from the carton.

"Can you get a glass please?" shouts Mum.

"I'm off now," he announces.

"Can't you wait for your sister?" And then she spots my eyes,

"M, are you wearing make-up to school?"

"It's the last day. We're allowed." And I have applied *Skylar's Smoky Eyes. A sure fire way of getting noticed by the boy you want!*

"It's lovely but..." And Toby burps.

"Toby!" shouts Mum and he laughs. Mum tuts and says, "Why don't you walk in together?"

"No, I've got to get in early and set up the main hall for some end of term thing... Hey M, why don't you go wild and have a JAM sandwich?"

"Muuum," I say, "tell him!"

"I think he's attempting a joke M."

"Yeah, lighten up Sis."

I only eat *cheese* sandwiches – in fact I only eat six other types of food: chicken, fruit, rice, yogurts, cake and cereal. I've never tried any other kind of sandwich and I don't want to. This is what I know and this is what I expect. And why is he doing this? I can feel I am going red, **BURNING**, and I swear I can feel anxiety enter our little house.

"It's a joke M!" and he drains the carton of juice.

"Toby, you are NOT to drink from the carton!" she yells and he throws it in the bin because it's empty now and he leaves the room muttering,

"What's the point of dirtying a glass...?"

And then Mum does the illogical thing she always does and shouts after him when he can't possibly hear,

"We don't want your germs Toby! Thank you very much. Just use a glass!"

And all this shouting and winding me up is cruel and last days are very difficult as it is, especially the last day of term before Christmas.

People unravel and so do I.

I plead with Mum to let me take the day off.

"Muuuum, pleeeasse. I don't want to go in. Pleeeasse..."

I wince as she **BANGS** a cereal bowl and spoon on the kitchen table and Anxiety marches in and pulls at me.

She shakes Rice Pops into the bowl... Bella hoovers up the few that escape on to the floor.

"I caaaaan't go in today. It's a horrible day."

"Oh come on M. The last day is a short day and then you have two weeks of freedom. You can't miss school because you don't *fancy* it." She opens a fresh carton of orange juice and pours it into my glass. The liquid dazzles me. Bella nuzzles into me. "Go away Bella, let M have her breakfast in peace." And she shoos Bella away, but I like my dog being close. Her gentle presence softens the edges of my life.

"Eat your breakfast."

"Buuuut nooooo." And it's not a case of not *fancying* it. The timetable will have collapsed today because it is a half day.

Anxiety breathes heavily in my ear and pushes at me.

Time will have collapsed. Bella thankfully returns to my side.

Mum is now stirring her coffee, loudly.

"Can you just stop that?" And I indicate to her stirring.

"It's just a spoon M! God, you're not in a good mood are you?"

I watch as she tries to stir quietly.

"Is there a specific problem M?" And then she stops and looks me directly in the eyes. I drop my head. "Is it something to do with Shaznia?"

"Noooooo." And I push the cereal away.

"Well, what then?"

"It's the timetable… It's all different."

"So the timetable will have changed? Is that the problem? Oh come on M, you have to be more flexible than this." And she pushes the bowl back to me. "You can't go to school on an empty stomach."

But what I am trying to say is time will have no meaning for me today.

Today I have no hold on time.

I will be adrift in the universe as anxiety pummels at me and shakes me and teases and tortures me.

My little squares of "timetable time" won't work. The time is all broken up and sharp timetable lines are jutting out and piercing space.

I have nothing to apply to time.

A vast, scary unknowingness is opening up ahead of me which I cannot measure or feel, like other people seem to.

Time does not hold me warmly in its arms. No, it drops me from a height and I fall, and fall like Alice in Wonderland down, down the big black hole, but I'm not in Wonderland. I'm in a harshly lit council-run school in Sevenoaks. That stinks of disinfectant and is held together with a series of unfriendly corridors.

The little timetable squares help me traverse the noises and smells and people.

Without them I am truly lost and a school day becomes an eternity, and I want to ask Mum how she would react if eternity lay ahead of her today? How scary would that be??? But instead I push my breakfast away again and say,

"I doooon't want to go innnn…"

"Come on M. One spoonful please M."

Bella flops to the kitchen floor and sighs and watches me as I force cereal down my throat.

"You have to be strong, M!" And she grabs one of her magnets from the fridge and reads out,

WOMEN ARE LIKE TEABAGS. YOU NEVER
KNOW HOW STRONG THEY ARE TILL
YOU PUT THEM IN HOT WATER.

I hate this fridge magnet. I hate it. I hate it above all the other fridge magnets of nonsense stuck on that stupid fridge. It makes no sense and sounds ridiculous. I push my luminous orange juice away. She **SLAMS** the magnet back on top of Toby's Most Polite Boy Certificate and grabs another and reads,

CHALLENGES ARE LIFE'S GYM.
THEY MAKE YOU STRONGER.

"Oh Muuuuuum!" I shout. "I doooon't waaaant to go!" I hardly slept the night before worrying about the surprise Mr Bray said was happening. I'm exhausted. "Muuuuumm…please."

"Honey. You have to go in."

"Buuut I don't want toooo."

"M, stop. Stop it." And I'm slipping into a MEltDOwN. Mum has moved the furniture round to fit the Christmas tree, in the little space we have. The fairy lights are flashing. Flashing. Flashing. She's wrapped tinsel round the banisters and the pictures and all I can smell is the tree. We are currently living with a tree inside our house!

"Muuuuummm. You said if I am ill I don't have to go to school…you saaaaid."

"You're not ill M. You're having a meltdown aren't you? Oh no, please. Not now. "

"I doooon't want to go innnnn…" And I want to scream at her. Has she forgotten about the leaflets and websites about autism and meltdowns? Why did she push me into this? I feel provoked into this. I am trying to fight it but I've slipped into the control of The Beast and I am so filled with rage and frustration and fear all I can do is cry out,

"I want to staaay home."

"Can you not, just for once, please stop this? Can you just do this for me M? Please. I can't be late for work today."

"Muuummm. I waaaant to stay here…"

"Please, for me – try! Can't you *try* and pull it together? All the things I do for you and I am asking you, this once, to just try and stop this!"

And I try to take deep breaths but Anxiety's hands are gripping my throat and I am choking, and if I can't breathe I'll die, and I gasp for air and tears are rolling, hot, down my cheeks. I shake.

She sits down opposite me. Her tone of voice is different. I can't work out if it's sad, frustrated or resentful. Maybe it's all three, but her voice is quieter and that's a good thing.

"Take a deep breath." And I follow the instructions. "In and out…in and out. Remember what Fiona said about breathing. It calms you."

Anxiety's grip loosens, allowing me to breathe a little air into my lungs.

And I think about how one day I'll own a fridge and I'll put magnets on it and they will have very clear, helpful messages on them, like,

BE QUIET!

LET ME FINISH MY SENTENCE.

SAY EXACTLY WHAT YOU MEAN.

"In and out." And Mum reaches across the table to take my hand and I pull away, and Mum keeps her hand on the table – reaching out to me – and a void as deep and wide as the Atlantic Ocean opens up between us. She will never know how I am and how I feel. And she reaches her hand out a little further to me and I can't take it because I do NOT want to carry her stain, her imprint, round with me all day.

I know it upsets her and that makes Anxiety creep towards me again.

"Keep breathing M. Take a deeper breath… And release." She draws her hand back, slowly, and places it on her lap.

And I breathe in and out.

Anxiety backs out the room and I've done it. I've pulled myself out of a meltdown. I'm still teetering on the edge and I know Anxiety is hanging around the hall or sneaking about upstairs, but for now I have some release.

Mum gets up and pours me a glass of water.

WATER and AIR. Two basic things in life seem to help. They're not complicated. If only I could remember to keep it as basic as water and air…

"What I was trying to say before you had a…one of these…is I think you need to be brave today."

"Think?" I question.

"You *need* to go to school today and be brave. It's a half day, so when you come home you can lie down and have a rest. School finishes at midday. So you will be home by 1.00." I appreciate the instructions and I do feel much calmer, although I do feel like I could flare UP and tip into a MEltDOwN again very easily. She hands me my school bag, containing my Christmas cards to give out and my present for

Shaznia. And I wonder if I'll see Lynx today because I won't get to see him leave History at the end of a Friday like I normally do. This half day/last day is practically ruining my life.

Mum drags a letter out of the drawer. I watch and she sees me.

"It's nothing M."

"Is it about me?"

"No… It's…it's from the solicitor…just about sorting out things between me and your dad."

And I take a deep breath and focus on not tipping into a meltdown. A strong, deep breath to bring myself away from its pull.

She sighs, then puts on a very poor Spanish accent and says, "We'll have fajitas for dinner! Toby's out, so just you, me and Bella. Girls night in, eh?"

And I wonder if Mum really cares. I mean *really* cares. All the leaflets, all the websites, go on about *"meltdowns being a defining feature of autism."* I sometimes wonder if Mum really believes this is all happening to us.

christmas, a sparkly, spiky threat that looms at the end of every year and a sinister santa who knows what I've been doing and knows where I have been.

★ Chapter 6 ★

Buying the Christmas card for Shaznia really felt like one of the best moments of my life. One of the most normal moments. Walking into The Card Emporium and buying your best friend a card. Simple and fun. It was a castle on a snow-topped mountain, but all the snow was pink glitter, and the message said:

Happy Sparkly Christmas Best Friend
You deserve all the glitter and
joy a girl can have!

It is very reassuring for our friendship to be official and clear.

When I was in The Card Emporium buying Shaznia's card and cinnamon scented candle I looked at all the cards for boyfriends! A whole section of cards dedicated to your boyfriend.

My gorgeous boyfriend. My sexy boyfriend. My hunky man (!!!!!!!!!).

And next to them was the Fiancé section and then it was the Husband section! And I dreamed of me sending one of these to Lynx next Christmas... And I got so excited that this could be my future one day!

Future! Future? Future? And I feel unease but then the thought of a Boyfriend, Fiancé, Husband.

What a truly wonderful order of life!

I actually skipped and let out a squeal of excitement at the thought of sending one of these cards to Lynx one day!!!! And as I walked through The Card Emporium I could see engagement cards and wedding cards and anniversaries of Silver, Gold and Ruby and then the Deepest Sympathy cards and my mood dropped. I felt really sad. Mum had to explain to me what this meant when Grandad died and we received lots of Deepest Sympathy cards.

And I thought about the order of life and how The Card Emporium sums life up.

And then I saw a very small section labelled DIVORCE. I picked one up and read

Congratulations on your Divorce (and not having to pretend you like your in-laws)

Mum doesn't like her in-laws and I don't think she ever pretended, so I won't buy her this card, if they get divorced. But I'm not sure where Mum and Dad's separation fits into all of this series of life events... I don't see any Separation cards, so where do I fit in? Where does my cracked-up little family fit in all of this? Maybe they will get divorced and I feel bad, sad and heavy that I caused this. So many happy events and then Deepest Sympathy and Divorce. Loss. But Ruby anniversaries and weddings too!

Life is full of so many UPs and downS.

Shaznia's card to me was Rudolph with a red, woolly bobble for his nose and she'd wrapped a pair of really cool mittens from Topshop, but the card didn't say anything about being my friend in it.

A bomb exploded when Mr Bray announced that the surprise was the staff performing a carol concert for us in the Main Hall, lesson 2. The class roared and groaned and Mr Bray shouts,

"Quiet down 8B!"

The timetable has collapsed. Time was officially broken and defunct. Order has escaped through the fractures and cracks and now HAVOC!

MONDAY	TUESDAY	WEDNESDAY	THURSDAY	FRIDAY
Maths	Geography	English	French	Art
Art	Maths	English	PSE	Art
Science	French	RE	Geography	PSE
Science	RE	Maths	Maths	French
LUNCH LUNCH LUNCH				
History	English	PE	English	PSE
French	PSE	History	English	Drama

I tap my face. Joe, who is sitting next to me, says,

"Meet you on the other side of this living hell."

Living hell. He is right, and I know it's a perfect opportunity for The Beast to hunt me down, find me and embark on a frenzied attack.

But I breathe deeply.

IN and OUT because the one good thing that comes from all this disorder, the one good thing is I get to sit next to Shaznia as our surnames start with the same letter.

PLUS

A full school assembly means seeing Lynx. Juicy-lipped, hair-gelled, sparkly eyes with a dewy complexion, Lynx.

And I cling on to the thought of seeing him.

Deep breath in.

And breathe out.

Lynx Lynx Lynx Lynx Lynx Lynx Lynx Lynx Lynx Lynx Lynx Lynx Lynx Lynx Lynx Lynx Lynx Lynx

His soft cheeks and gelled hair gives me focus amongst all the glitter and chaos. Shaznia collapses and flops in the seat next to me with all her bags and coat and says,

"God I hate all this!"

Why would she hate all this? She gets to sit next to me, her friend, so I ask her and she says,

"Errrr...I hate that I have to watch old teachers sing carols badly."

Maybe she doesn't want to be my friend any more and the thought circles **round and round** my head because her card didn't say anything about being my friend. I think about what Fiona has said about getting obsessive.

"If you are having a repetitive thought, interrupt it with a healthy positive thought. Stop them from taking over. You are in control M. You are in charge." So I think about Bella wagging her tail and I smile to myself.

"What are you smiling at M?" asks Shaznia. "Weirdo."

"I was just thinking about Bella."

"Awwww. I love Bella! Can I come over and see her?"

"Sure...I'm not a weirdo," I say. Shaznia ignores this.

"Over Christmas?"

"Yes," I reply and I want to ask, what day? What time? But then she starts to play with my hair.

"I love your hair M." I tolerate the discomfort, for my friendship. I really am wearing my friendship mask right now. With every stroke of my hair she is leaving her stain on me. I have to pull away. "So shiny. Have you put a colour in it?"

"Yes, it's called Gorgeous Shimmer."

"And your eye make-up is so pretty."

"Oh it's from Skylar's Guide to Doing Christmas Right! It's the toned-down version of smoky party eyes."

"Will you do mine like that?"

"Sure!" I reply. "If you come and see Bella I can get all the colours and brushes ready." And I want to know when exactly will she visit, but then she squeals,

"Yea!" And claps her hands.

"Yea!" I copy and clap my hands and I worry, what day she will visit? And I'm not a weirdo...am I?!

Mr Crane, the Head, is a tall, slow man with lots of angles and he looks a bit like some kind of bird. He is a...measured man. All his footsteps are the same distance and he wears the same shirt and tie on the same days every week. Today is Friday and he is wearing his blue shirt and a beige, checked tie. And he is not very friendly. He appears on the stage and tells us all to be quiet and everyone stops talking but it's not quiet. Chairs scrape, teachers whisper, sick people cough…and then off-key singing begins.

The carol concert was painful but I don't think that had anything to do with my autism. I think the teachers thought they were being young and they're just not. I think they think acting young makes them popular. It doesn't – they are old and we need old people. So why aren't they just proud of that? I need older people to help me, guide and tell me what to do sometimes. Not sing a rap song, in a Christmas carol style, when I should be in double art.

Shaznia kept looking back at Lynx and his best mate Jake.

"What's Lynx doing?" I whispered.

"Errr, he's kind of looking over at us."

Lynx Lynx Lynx Lynx Lynx Lynx Lynx Lynx Lynx Lynx Lynx Lynx Lynx Lynx Lynx Lynx Lynx Lynx

"KIND OF! What does KIND OF mean?" I turn and he *is* looking. He blushes! I blush and I turn back to face the teachers ruining Silent Night. OMG! This is the first step to a steady relationship! That's what it says in *Cherry Magazine*, The Flirt Issue!

Eye contact is the best way to know if he's interested in you, and if your boy blushes this could be love!!!

The teachers do a particularly flat version of a song by some men called Simon and Garfunkel, called The Sound of Silence. Obviously writing about silence, then making a noise about it, doesn't make sense and is confusing, but right now the most important thing is that Lynx looked at me! Maybe it was my smoky eyes that did it. Like Skylar says, *Smoky eyes are a sure fire way to getting noticed by the boy you want.* It works!!!!

I'm buzzing! My senses are heightened!

Lynx Lynx Lynx Lynx Lynx Lynx Lynx Lynx Lynx Lynx Lynx Lynx Lynx Lynx Lynx Lynx Lynx Lynx

Eventually the singing is mercifully over and we can leave the echoing hall and headache-inducing lights. No one is in register order any more.

All the years are м=uₐDₗ-eₐ up and out of oerdr.

As we file out of the hall for the last time this year, I scan the room looking for Lynx. I can smell the high notes of Lynx body spray. The muddle has brought him nearer to me. Amber Jade is mixed amongst all the other deodorants and perfumes but I can identify this scent. Amber Jade.

But instead of Lynx, Joe appears by my side and is talking about how he now thinks he has permanent inner ear damage, which he closely follows up with the word "joke." (Not funny to joke about life-debilitating medical conditions.) And I trace the Amber Jade and see Lynx talking to Shaznia! And I want to rush over and talk too but I can't because the lights are buzzing and there are too many people in the way and I hate the way I am! I hate it! And I feel angry! Raging! Why can't I just go up to them and be like everyone else!!! All the other pretty girls in Sevenoaks! Pretty girls who effortlessly chit-chat! And small talk.

And then he disappears…disappears into Christmas. Off to his wonderful Amber-Lynx scented world of Jade, Gold Temptation and White Peace…

Then Shaznia appears at my face,

"Are you *sure* you can't come up town hun?"

She asks me this question like she has asked me earlier and she hasn't asked me earlier. "I've got enough money to get you an eggnog latte." My stomach churns.

"I have to get home," I say. Which isn't a complete lie, so I'm not worried about another tape worm incident, but I can't because I know The Beast would be waiting for me in town. Pacing around the streets, sniffing me out to pounce on me and render me useless by the town fountain.

"Never mind," she replies quickly and backs out the hall saying, "Merry Christmas M! I'll text you over the holidays." And all I really want to do is throw my bag over my shoulder, re-do my smoky eyes, apply some more Pink Kisses lipstick and say,

"Sure, see you up there hun."

But I can't.

I am not like the other girls.

Joe says he'll walk home with me but I ask him why he doesn't go up town with the others. If I could,

I would, and he says that watching Shaznia drink an eggnog latte on a war memorial isn't his idea of fun. I think to myself how much I'd love it because it's about fitting in and having a choice.

Choice. That's what I want really.

I am controlled. Controlled by anxiety and my need to be prepared for every possible outcome, but that is an impossibility...so anxiety reigns over my life.

What was Shaznia talking about to Lynx?

Lynx Lynx Lynx Lynx Lynx Lynx Lynx Lynx Lynx Lynx Lynx Lynx Lynx Lynx Lynx Lynx Lynx Lynx

We walk out the school. I make up an excuse to check a notice board in the art block, so I can walk past the the coins and count:

1, 2, 3, 4, 5, 6, 7, 8, 9, 10, 11, 12

The half day meant I didn't have time to do my usual 12 times check. They are reassuringly still there and that's what I need on a half day/last day. We are walking along Vernon Road by The Money Shop.

The window display of diamond rings, gold chains and shiny watches changes a lot in The Money Shop.

People sell their precious items because they can't pay a bill, says Mum, and I think maybe they didn't have any choice either. Maybe they had to sell their rings and chains to pay their electricity bills and I know how sad that is, and the window becomes a very sad window of second-hand jewels... And then I shudder, thinking about all the stains, all the passed-on energy in these jewels.

But I like the big M in the sign.

As we walk Joe asks why I like Shaznia so much, and I explain that she is my friend, and he says he thinks she's a bit of a user. User. And then he asks why I call Lynx "Lynx" and I explain about Amber Jade, White Lines, Africa and all the other ranges of body spray which he wears, and he nods and asks,

"Did you get the card I gave you M?"

I did, and I recite the message on the front under the laughing snowman,

"Tis the season to be jolly!" And add, "Actually, Joe, I think 'Tis the season to shut yourself in your bedroom and breathe deeply,'" and he says he understands that very well and he wished he had a bedroom to shut himself away and he says I'm lucky. Lucky? How! How amazing that someone thinks *I* am lucky! We get to my house and Joe asks to come in and watch a film but I say no.

"I could take Bella round the block for you?" he suggests.

"Err…no, Joe."

"Is Toby about? I could say hi."

"No," I reply. "Toby is out. He's at the Christmas party, at the football club." And I am so glad he is out and I can be on my own.

"I have to go in now." And the truth is I should be in a French lesson right now anyway, so it's best I go in and try to cope with the displacement and broken afternoon.

"OK. Merry Christmas M. I'll call over in the holidays," he says as he walks up the road and I wonder *when* exactly. And that makes me feel edgy. Edgy. Will he *call* round? Or will he call me on my mobile? Will he give me warning? Maybe I should call him and tell him not to call round.

I turn the key in the door and enter my little, warm home.

The last day/half day has ended and I have made it. Term has ended and I survived!

I stand in the hall and enjoy feeling in one piece.

I can hear the fridge whirring but I feel a sense of calm and I am grateful for this moment.

Anxiety doesn't seem to be near. Perhaps it is waiting by the war memorial for me. Coming home was definitely the right decision.

Bella waddles up to me, wagging her tail, and I kneel down and hug her. Bella is the only one I hug. Hugs and kisses. She pulls away and walks to the back door and I let her in the garden. The apple tree's black twigs and branches are scoring the grey sky. Dark, spiky beauty, and I am settled by the cold air and the shadowy moon, which is beginning to show in the sky.

I can look at the moon for hours, sometimes. It is never stressed, even though it looks over some terrible situations. I breathe in nature's centring strength. Constant and full of magnificent systems that connect us all, and nature's brilliance calms me, further.

I go to my room, Bella follows and collapses on my bedside rug, and I look up USER.

User

[noun]

1. A person or thing that *uses*.

2. One who *uses* drugs, especially as an abuser or addict.

And I wonder why Joe has told me she is a user? We're all users. I'm a user but I'm certainly not a drug addict. Drug addict?

Why would Joe say Shaznia is a drug addict?

USER USER USER

Does Shaznia use me? And I feel rotten.

I look up photos of Lynx on the school football website and I go from rotting to sweetness. Inside I feel sweet and sparkly and I just really, really love him!

Athletic! Strong! Fit! Handsome!! Muscles! Legs!!! Lynx!

Action shots!

Lynx scoring a goal! GOAL!!!!!!

Team photos!

Holding a trophy, high above his head!

Photos on the school mini bus, "Off to win at Hollingbrook High."

Handsome, successful, juicy-lipped Lynx.

I look in the bedroom mirror and say, "All in all, M, this term was C minus."

And now I needed to sleep and let my masks drop.

Daughter

Friend

Student

Sister

Small talker

I lie on my little bed and be Me. I think about…

Mum and Dad

Lynx Lynx Lynx Lynx Lynx Lynx
Lynx Lynx Lynx Lynx Lynx Lynx
Lynx Lynx Lynx Lynx Lynx Lynx

Life has piled so much on top of me.

AN-Xiety

sep- ar- ation

Fractured time

FRIENDSHIP?

Lynx Lynx Lynx Lynx Lynx Lynx Lynx Lynx
Lynx Lynx Lynx Lynx Lynx Lynx Lynx Lynx
Lynx Lynx

Exhaustion consumes me. I could sleep through Christmas. I'd like to. Bella is already snoring.

I worry about the next two weeks of "freedom" – that's what everyone calls school holidays – and I worry about the unfolding days and events. How time bends and expands at Christmas and routines change and disintegrate.

Disintegrate and change! And Anxiety tweaks at me but even Anxiety cannot take on sleep right now. The need to close my smoky eyes and pull my purple and grey blanket around me tightly and sleep is greater than anxiety. I am so pleased that my body allows me to drift off… It isn't jerking with stress or racing with fear. My body is allowing me to fall into a beautiful, heavy sleep.

Christmas. Stressful and disappointment. I take to my room and avoid a Christmas sensory overload.

★ Chapter 7 ★

When I wake up the house feels different. Houses feel different at different times of the day, week or year. Friday night is a bit loose. Monday morning is stressed. Thursday evenings are unwinding, and Sunday evenings feel very, very empty. Days before Christmas, like this one, feel buzzy yet calm.

I can hear Dad's voice.

Dad brings a different presence to the house. A manly presence and a mixture of security and frustration. I look at my clock. It is 7.30. I have slept for 5 hours and 30 minutes and unusually I have been left to sleep.

I walk down the stairs, his voice getting louder, and with every step I realise just how much I've been missing him.

He and Mum are talking. Mum is going through Christmas cards and he is sitting on the sofa.

Right in the middle. That's where he always sits. Like he owns it, and I guess he does own half of it. The sofa always felt like it was Dad's. He had priority over it. Grandma called him Sofa Simon because she said he practically lived on it. She said he should have been out there trying to find work, not plucking a guitar all day long on the sofa, like a teenager.

"M!" he says and opens his arms as I walk in.

"I didn't know you were coming to visit," I say.

"Well, I'm just dropping some presents off and hoping we can arrange to meet up over Christmas?"

"I'm not going to The Oval," I state, quickly.

"Right…" and he looks down. Mum gets up and places some turquoise baubles on the tree and says,

"It's a stupid idea Simon."

"Nan would love to see you. She's getting old, you know."

"Are you trying to tell me she will be dead soon?" I ask. And I wonder if that's deliberately said to make me feel guilty. It feels a bit like the tape worm lie twitching or The Beast of Anxiety, creeping into the room.

"No, no! I hope not! Just well…well she's getting old M…so maybe I am saying that!"

Dad ended up sleeping on the sofa too and the sofa still has Dad's shapes in it...so in a funny way even though Dad doesn't live with us any more he still has a presence here.

When we had our last family holiday Dad slept on the sofa too. Poor Daddy. We went to the New Forest because Mum knows I love trees and nature and she said we would probably see some deer and foxes. She said Dad and Toby could go out cycling and we could go shopping and have cream teas. But it didn't really work out that way because of course Anxiety jumped in the car and travelled down with us. Mum described my anxiety as "off the scale" on that holiday. I don't know if there is an official anxiety scale, like the Richter Scale for earthquakes or the Volcano Explosivity Index. To be honest I don't really need an Anxiety Scale. The volcano one will do just fine.

1. non-explosive
2. gentle
3. severe
4. cataclysmic
5. paroxysmal
6. colossal
7. super-colossal
8. mega-colossal

So this scale only goes up to 8... So imagine how I was feeling when I was *off* the scale. I was feeling beyond mega-colossal. And I think that is a fair representation of how I felt.

Normally we go to Jackie's parents' cottage in Cornwall. I love it there because I am so used to it. I have been there every August since I was born and I have a system when we stay there. I know my room and I am allowed to get on with an order of events that make me feel safe. But Jackie's parents were having family over from America, so we couldn't stay that year, and applying the system to Sun Cottage in the New Forest didn't work. Mum said,

"Well, now we know...I suppose."

Dad brought one of his guitars and played it on the sofa most of the day, Toby went out and made lots of friends in the neighbouring cottages, and Mum tried to get me to go on a woodland nature trail and a beauty treatment day at Bay Tree Beauty Spa but I couldn't really leave my bedroom. Mum and Dad argued for the first two days and then Dad went to The Green Man pub and came home and fell asleep on the sofa. Mum cried a lot. I'm not sure if there is a tear scale but she would have been very high on it that week. Super, mega-colossal crying. And through Mum's tears I remember her saying,

"He just can't cope with you M and I can't cope with this situation any more."

And,

"Could you just try and be a bit more flexible, for the sake of the family M?"

And I thought if I could, believe me I would. Do you think I want to spend my holiday stuck in a room that smells of damp? But I couldn't get those words out.

Anxiety clung to me most of the week. It dragged out of me, its claws constantly scraping at my skin, or it would screech in my ear, tearing at my nerves. Lying in bed seemed the only way to manage it, control it. Sometimes Bella would lie in the room with me as I lay on my bed, wrapped tightly in the green and yellow blanket my mum made me, and I'd try to read a book, but Anxiety doesn't make that easy. Bella would scratch at the door to go out and sniff about the forest. Staying in a room for most of a holiday isn't something anyone or any animal would choose to do, but no one seemed to realise this.

There was one good thing about this holiday and no one else seemed to notice…which did entice me out of the room. In the morning the sun rose at the front of the house, and by the late evening the earth had spun around and I could watch the sun set in the back garden. There was a bench by the front door and the back door, where I would sit with Bella lying on the grass beside me. I am sure they must have been put there for the purpose of sun watching as I had a perfect line of vision, which meant I could see the first ray of sun and the final golden sliver of light in the evening, and then I would retreat back to my room. And holding on to these two regular, daily events helped me survive that week. I didn't know I had autism then, no one did, but I wondered if the person who put these benches in the perfect spot felt like me. And as my parents rowed and the tension rose, the deep fault lines began to show in our family, but I felt some comfort in knowing that someone shares my appreciation of the sun. Maybe, maybe there is someone else out there like me.

The car journey home was one of the most distressing times of my life. No one spoke and it was as if we all knew something was going to happen. CHANGE. Bella felt it too. She curled up in the space behind the back seats and sighed. She didn't try to jump over the back seats or steal our food when Toby got his sweets out.

Change was in the air.

Something about Mum had changed and it kept me off the scale. I was mega-mega-mega-mega-colossal off the scale. Anxiety had taken possession of me. A complete takeover of my mind and body. I just couldn't get it out of me. I was shaking the whole way home in the car. Toby just sat beside me, his ear phones on, looking out the window, and at Winchester Service Station on the M3 I heard Mum on her mobile saying,

"Yeah we've, well, *I've* decided Jacks, just got to do it. This can't go on. I can't go on like this…"

Dad pulled up outside our house and he didn't get out of the car. Mum, me and Toby did. Mum opened the boot and Bella jumped out and stretched and walked up to the front door. She looked over her shoulder to watch us all follow but we didn't *all* follow this time. We took our bags from the boot. Toby went to take Dad's out and Mum put her hand on the bag and said,

"No, leave it."

Dad did finally get out of the car with the engine still running and said,

"I'll see you in a few days, at the weekend kids, yeah?"

And Toby said,

"Why? What's going on?"

And Dad gave Toby a hug and he went to give me a hug but I stepped back, and he looked at Mum and said,

"See, she won't even let me hug her."

And he got in the car, **SLAMMED** the door and drove off, and we all stood and watched him turn right into Clement Road and he was gone.

"Where's he going? Mum, what's going on?" And fury seemed to arrive in Toby and his face wasn't happy. His face grew redder and redder and he was shouting, "Where's he going? Mum?" And I can't read emotions well but I recognised that my brother was very distressed.

"Just come in and we'll talk." And she tried to loop her arm around Toby's and he pulled his arm away and shouted,

"No! Where's he gone? Tell me Mum. Is he coming back?"

"Come on Toby. Ssssshhh." And she walked towards the front door. "Come on!"

"Has he left us Mum?" And she said,

"No, no. Let's get inside and let's all talk."

But Toby would not follow these instructions and Bella was barking and jumping up at him, and he kept shouting,

"I hate you."

Hate hate hate hate

His arms were flailing all over the place as Mum grabbed his arm and said,

"Please Toby. In the house – now!"

I had to cover my ears as Mum pulled him by his faded orange t-shirt along the path. She dropped her plastic bags and a wellington boot and suntan lotion bottles fell all over the flower bed. And although I've always felt Toby's anger, just under the surface of his skin, I'd never seen him release it out into the world before, into our little garden, and sweep along our quiet little street, disturbing neighbours and bringing them out of their front doors.

Dereck from next door appeared and said,

"Everything all right Amanda?"

And Mum replied,

"Yes, Dereck. It's all fine."

As she pulls Toby nearer the front door and he is shouting at her and saying, "Why can't we just be a normal family?" I think, is this fine? How can this be fine? If this is fine, how can I trust anything? Any feelings? Anything my mum says? Finally Toby got in the house and we sat at the kitchen table. Toby's arms are folded tight and his red face is turned towards the back door.

Mum explains that Dad is staying at Nan's, for a while, at The Oval and I said,

"I'm not going to The Oval."

And Mum said I didn't have to go there, and Toby asked,

"Why?"

And Mum explained that things were getting difficult, and Toby said,

"It's because of her, isn't it? It's her fault we can't be a proper family because she never wants to do things or leave her room and can't you all see there is something wrong with her?"

And Mum said,

"It's not easy. You know we've been to countless doctors and meetings and I am desperate to find out what the matter is. I am really trying to sort out this problem!"

Problem

And they were talking about me like I wasn't there, and I wanted to ask, "How long is a while?" Is it a metre? Is it 20 years? Is it more like grams or millilitres? I just don't know! What do you mean a while? When *exactly* is Dad coming back home? But I can't talk and I go to my room and look up **while.**

While
[noun]

1. An interval of time: To wait a long while; he arrived a short while ago.

It really doesn't help. Dad might be away for a long while or a short while... Lots of metres or a small amount of metres? Lots of hours or years? I close my eyes and imagine I am orbiting in the peace of space, floating around the planetary system, and this becomes another of my MOLW. My Own Little World. Safe and solitary, and I put myself here away from all this terror and confusion.

Toby hasn't been at home much since that day and Dad hasn't come home, to live. Three weeks later, on a Monday when we were at school, he cleared out his records, guitars and clothes.

But he still has his shape on the sofa and I quite like that.

I'm trying to take steps in the right direction but it's very hard to even keep a foot on the ground.

★ Chapter 8 ★

I am pleased to see Dad. Especially when he says,

"No of course you don't have to come to The Oval."

I know I don't throw my arms around him, kiss him all over the face and say, "Pop! Pop! You're the best!" like Skylar in the final scene of Family Ties, season 6, episode 2, but I do love him and miss him very much. I think I probably get on better with him now he is at The Oval. Our house is quite little, so we were all CRAMMED into the small rooms with all Dad's records and guitars and all the tension was rammed and piled, squeezed and crammed into our little home, and it always felt like the roof might blow off or doors would burst off the hinges. There is tension in the room again. A very particular tension between my mum and dad – Toby said it's an angry-frustrated-irritated tension that they create. I'm not very good at identifying it but it is uncomfortable to be in.

"Well, I thought we could make some plans for the Christmas holiday. I know you...like to plan." And think this really is a change (for the good – and I rarely think that!!!). Dad seems to be acknowledging I need to plan! I wonder if he's been reading some websites about autism or a book. So we sit at the kitchen table and Dad produces a blank piece of paper and a pen. Mum says,

"I don't want M tiring herself out."

And,

"I'm going out with Jackie on New Year's Eve, so don't mess up those plans."

Dad ignores her and says,

"OK M. Write down a list of things we could do."

I stare at the blank, empty piece of paper.

"I'll make a cup of tea and give you some space." And he makes a cup of tea and him and Mum talk about a credit card bill. The tension rises.

Dad sits back down. The paper is still blank and there are things I'd like to do, like see Shaznia and go on a date with Lynx, but that's not doing things with Dad.

"She's exhausted Simon," says Mum, adding more turquoise baubles to the tree, and she's right. I do want to do something, but this term has left me spent and this exercise, this game, is highlighting my inabilities even more. Dad picks up the pen and writes:

Christmas shopping

Cinema

Pantomime

Drive to the seaside

Walk Bella

And he hands me the pen and says put a cross by any of those that you'd like to do while Mum is now talking about ice-skating and Christmas Choco-Mochas at the new coffee shop.

And I put a big ✗ by "Walk Bella" and Dad grabs Bella's lead from the banisters and says, "Come on then," and Bella jumps up and can't believe it. An extra walk.

"You too M," says Dad. "Let's go round the block."

Mum lights some gold, frankincense candles as we leave, and normally I don't like "just doing things" without planning, but in a way we have planned this walk and I have had some say in it. That can make a huge difference to me.

We walk along our road and right into Clement Road. The road Dad disappeared down when he left that day.

Bella is pulling. Stopping. Sniffing. We walk past lots of houses, with trees with flashing lights wound round their trunks and branches...as if they are not beautiful enough, I think.

And Dad does small talk about school and Nan, and I nod and feel annoyed as I am enjoying the bright, chilly evening, but then he says,

"You know, you can ask me anything M."

And I like this. Direct. We walk along Orchard Drive, so I say,

"Dad, I do have a question."

"Great M. Great. Anything."

"Why is Orchard Drive called Orchard Drive and there are only two trees on this road? And two trees do not make an orchard, plus they are not fruit trees."

"I suppose there must have been an orchard here...years ago."

We keep walking and Dad suggests we walk round the long way, past the park, and I agree as it is a clear night and nobody is around. It is still and quiet and Dad has stopped small talking now. It's very unusual to go on a walk with Dad. He never used to take Bella out. It was me, Mum or Toby. He'd just sit on the sofa and play riffs on his guitars or listen to albums of The Smiths or The Cocteau Twins. This is new. This is nice.

Bella is pulling on the lead as we near the front door.

"Dad."

"Yes M."

"Can I ask you any question?"

"Anything."

"Is Turquoise blue or green?"

"Errr. I have to admit I don't know the answer to that question. I guess you can ask me anything but I won't always know the answer."

We arrive at our house and what I really want to know is how can I fix the family and I wonder if Mum and Dad should go on a "Date Night" like in Family Values, season 7, episode 4, when Skylar's parents go to Le Papillon and rekindle their love. So I say,

"Why don't you and Mum go to a French restaurant?"

And Dad starts asking lots of questions like,

"Did she suggest that?" and "Has she said anything about moving back together?"

And then I worry that he might come back with all his STUFF and we'd all live in a tiny, cramped house, all on top of each other. Rammed and crammed and shouting and that angry-frustrated-irritated tension that they create. And then I wonder if some relationships should be broken like in Skylar, season 13, episode 5, "Clean Break." When Skylar ends a relationship with Bud, her high school sweetheart, from her home town. She ends the episode saying, "Sometimes goodbyes are for the best." And her and Bud cry, but everything's all right now because Bud is training to be a lawyer at Harvard and she is a Super Teen pop sensation, in love with Ewan, her *true* love.

And Dad is still asking, "Has she said anything about me and her sorting things out?"

"No," I reply and he lets out a big breath. "She hasn't said any of those things." Mum swings the front door open.

"Where have you three been?" And Bella barges past her.

"We went the long way round," says Dad.

"It's freezing. Get in M. Simon, you shouldn't keep her out. It's so cold."

And Dad comes over four times over the Christmas holiday, for a walk around the long block. He calls me the day before and arrives at the arranged time. It's simple and straightforward and very enjoyable, and I was allowed to get on with sleeping and watching Skylar (and looking up pictures of Lynx).

There's a party in another room and I'm not invited but that's OK...I'll get some peace.

★ Chapter 9 ★

And the snow fell over the log cabin, a blanket of glistening white. A wolf padded through the Utah forest, past the log cabin, and inside a fire crackled and glowed as Skylar and Ewan sipped champagne, cuddled up on the cosy sofa. Romantic and safe.

Season 5, episode 7, Skylar Christmas special

Again

And the snow fell over the log cabin, a blanket of glistening white. A wolf padded through the Utah forest, past the log cabin, and inside a fire crackled and glowed as Skylar and Ewan sipped champagne, cuddled up on the cosy sofa. Romantic and safe.

Season 5, episode 7, Skylar Christmas special

Again

And the snow fell over the log cabin, a blanket of glistening white. A wolf padded through the Utah forest, past the log cabin –

But the scene is interrupted by laughing and crashing around downstairs – Mum and Jackie have been out and have now put loud music on too. I'd spent most of the holiday in my room, going over the term and looking at my card from Shaznia, which didn't say anything about being my friend. I lay on my bed and thought about Lynx and looked at the school football website and saw on his Facebook page that he was watching a match and eating a pizza with Jake.

Lynx Lynx Lynx Lynx Lynx Lynx Lynx Lynx Lynx Lynx Lynx

How I long to eat pizza and watch a match with Lynx.

I was also watching Skylar and avoiding doing things on the "List of Fun Christmassy Things to Do!" that Mum had left on my bed.

Fun Christmassy Things To Do!!!!

Christmas shopping

Ice skating with Toby

Drink gingerbread lattes

To get our nails done, all sparkly

Boxing Day drinks with Dereck and Sheila next door

They had turned the music up and were now shouting over it and Bella is barking. I couldn't concentrate on the season 5, episode 7, Skylar Christmas special. I went downstairs and told them to be quiet, which made them laugh lots, but being noisy at 11.00pm isn't funny at all. Jackie said,

"Oh M! It's so lovely to see you! We'll turn it down!"

But she didn't become quieter, at all. In fact I think they got noisier. Mum was trying to unscrew the cap off a bottle of wine and kept saying,

"Jacks, you are my best, bestest friend."

And she handed Jackie the bottle to undo and took one of her stilettos off. Jackie couldn't undo the bottle top either because she was trying to text whilst telling my mum she was the best friend ever. I could see Mum was on the edge of tears and I don't want her to be sad and cry, so I said,

"I think you've both had quite enough wine."

Which for some reason made them giggle again.

"Jacks, this is the best night I've had since university. I love it." Jackie managed to unscrew the lid and was now pouring out two large glasses of wine.

"I love going out! Mate!" And she hugs Jackie but stumbles because she is wearing one high heel. Mum is about to tip into sobbing. I can tell.

"You need to put that wine away, now, Mum."

Jackie snorts and Mum giggles.

"Oh stop M! I'm just letting my hair down with me old mate!" Jackie is now sitting on the sofa trying to focus on her phone and the FLASH FLASH FLASH of the tree lights disturb me.

"Who are you texting Jacks?" Mum asks, limping over to her.

"Jane and Helen." And then Jackie turns to me and says, "You know our uni friends. Jane was a scream."

A scrEam? She sounds awful.

"But I never really liked Helen," says Jackie, and I wonder why would you have a friend you don't like?

Then panicked, Mum asks,

"Where's Toby?"

"He's out! You drop[ ]

earlier," I said.

"Oh yeah!" And she [ ]

"How can you not re[ ]

"Come and have a cuc[ ]

my baby daughter."

I go back up to my r[ ]

I want is a cuddle or a lau_.., ~~~ actually the thing I

want most in the world is a cuddle and laugh.

And she's just not taking things seriously. Like my

autism. She was delighted when we got the diagnosis.

She was reading books and web pages and talked

about us going to meetings and then she just seemed

to stop. Like she stopped believing I had autism or

maybe when the reality of it began to unfold it all

became too difficult.

Like all those bills and solicitors letters she shoves in

the drawer. She puts them out of sight. Shoves them

away.

But I've been carrying it around with me my

whole life. That is my reality, and does she realise

how difficult that is? I think she's ignoring it but

I can't ignore it. And why would she ignore it? Why

don't people want to believe it?

And I am de[ ]

has a friend

not sur[ ]

ply, deeply upset that even my mum and they are texting more friends and I'm I have one friend.

And I hate texting or calling but I pick up my phone and type out,

Hi Shaznia, R U Still my friend? M

SEND

And I am so worried now, maybe I didn't look after our friendship because I couldn't go up town on the last day of term.

Anxiety scratches at me.

I decide to watch the opening scene of Skylar, season 5, episode 7, Skylar Christmas special, again and again.

347 views.

I check my phone.

412 views.

And still she hasn't texted me back. It's 1.50am. Maybe she is asleep.

Mum and Jackie are talking in hushed, low voices. Finally they are quiet! And I sit at the top of the stairs. Curious as to their tone of voice, which makes no sense to me.

And I've tried, *really* tried to understand the tones. Maybe it is like learning another language? But what I have learnt is that:

Friends can be loud and shout.

Friends can be quiet and practically inaudible.

But working out when and why has escaped me. I think it's all part of the friendship code. Which I haven't cracked. How do you know when to be quiet and when to be loud?

I check my phone. Still no reply.

And even though the truth is I love being on my own, I feel a desire to fit in and have friends. Like it's part of my purpose on earth. I'm hardwired to fit in! So I *try* to crack THE FRIENDSHIP CODE because if I don't crack the code, how will I ever get a boyfriend or a husband or have children? And I study *Cherry Magazine's* "How To Tell If She's A Real Friend" because I don't want to be completely on my own for ever and ever. I want to be accepted by my fellow human beings, but it really is so much easier on my own, and I retreat back to my little pink room, back to the security of my bed and blanket and the comfort of Skylar, season 5, episode 7, Skylar Christmas special again and again.

Dates. So much uncertainty! Will it last? Where will it go? What will happen? So much pressure.

⭐ Chapter 10 ⭐

Miracles Happen! This is the title of Skylar, season 9, episode 5, when Ewan arrives from the heavens in a private jet and sweeps Skylar off to the Greek Island of Cephalonia for dinner on the beach! And she declares,

"This is heaven on earth!"

And that is how I feel as I walk along Vernon Drive! A miracle has happened! And I know it's not as exotic as a Greek island and they have olive trees and in Sevenoaks we have...oaks and other equally beautiful trees, and they have glorious days of sunshine and today it is drizzling, but I couldn't be happier! It is as if I am dancing along the shore of a bright blue sea!

Oh God do I want this?

Shaznia came up to me on the first day back and I wasn't happy. I asked why she hadn't come round, as planned.

"Oh M! Christmas was crazy busy! And my aunt was ill and I had to visit her in hospital. It was really stressful."

And I feel guilty, but then not too guilty as I don't like her aunt very much.

"But you never texted me back?!"

"Oh God! I got a new phone and all my numbers and names got all muddled and the phone deleted some and –"

"You could have got my number and –"

"Oh M! Will you shut up honey! I've got something amazing to tell you! You are going to love me for ever and ever." And she told that she had arranged a date! A double date. Her and Jake. Me and Lynx! LYNX!!!!

I think I might turn back...yeah...go home.

But I can't turn back because this is all I want! I want a husband, children and a house, a honeymoon in Cephalonia, so I have to go on a date, so I can take a step in the right direction.

But I like being on my own. I love being on my own.

Shaznia arranged it at the New Year's Eve party.

And why wasn't I invited?

And Lynx said he thought I was really pretty. (Smoky eyes! Smoky eyes!) And Shaznia said she would arrange a meeting if he brought Jake along. So that's how it happened! My first ever double date! My first ever date!

I cannot do this. Anxiety is pacing behind me on Vernon Drive. I take a few deep breaths and it backs off.

I clap, clap, clap my hands, as I walk past The Money Shop, and I tell myself to stop clapping my hands. I think I may have let out a buzz or a little squeal as a girl at the bus stop looks up as I pass. But it's because inside my head Lynx and I are on honeymoon in Cephalonia! We are walking hand in hand and barefoot through the white sand of a beach! And then I skip and nearly trip on a Kent County Council crooked, cracked paving stone. Crooked and cracked. I am scared that I am not in charge of myself today.

Past the Moroccan Restaurant. I should turn round because what am I thinking? Me going on a date with someone as gorgeous as Lynx.

But I can't let Shaznia down. She's arranged this and I can't let Lynx down. All this effort for me! I have to go. But why a cinema? This would never be my idea for a first date. I wish we were going for a relaxing walk in the park or a café! Yes, a chilled café, but instead we are meeting at a loud, dark, big cinema. I want a boyfriend. Like the ones in The Card Emporium. My Hunky Boyfriend!!!!!

I must do this! I am doing what typical teenage girls do. I am typical!! I like being typical. Mum asked where I was going and I didn't lie (exactly), I said I was meeting Shaznia at the cinema. I didn't want to tell her about Lynx – she would definitely cause a fuss.

Fuss

[noun]

An excessive display of anxious attention or activity; needless or useless bustle.

No fuss. I don't want any fuss or useless bustle.

SaM's Chicken Shop

I can do this. I can move forward to a double date and a normal existence. And I count my steps in a series of 12.

1–2–3–4–5–6–7–8–9–10–11–12 and again. Be brave M! Come on girl!

How can a date be so exciting yet so terrifying? Does he know I have autism? I know I look the same as everyone else – better really. But does he know? I haven't told anyone at school. The teachers know. The information could have got out! Maybe he does know and still he wants to go out with me! Do I look like I have autism? Do my eyes tell people? Does the way I walk show I have autism? I flap and tap my cheeks at school and I try, desperately, to control it, but does that equal autism?

1–2–3–4–5–6–7–8–9–10–11–12 and again.

I decide to walk and not get the bus. The bus is very difficult. I like aisle seats. Will I get an aisle seat at the cinema?

My pink and white Vans are getting wet but I keep going. I have arranged, with myself, that I am to get to the date meeting point half an hour early because to risk being late for something as important as this would be harmful to me and Anxiety would most definitely catch up with me and attack.

1–2–3–4–5–6–7–8–9–10–11–12.

January! Oh January, people keep calling you bleak and a difficult month! But I have never been in light more beautiful than a low, silvery January late afternoon.

1–2–3–4–5–6–7–8–9–10–11–12 and again.
1–2–3–4–5–6–7–8–9–10–11–12 and again.

And I will wear my date mask and say, just like Skylar, "So good to see you." But then she kisses him on the lips. I don't want to do that. I'm not ready to kiss him. I AM ready to kiss him, but I can't! I flap my hands. A passenger on the passing 289 bus looks up from their phone. I press my hands on my side.

Date Mask! Date Mask!

Anxiety is catching up on me as I turn into the next street.

Deep breath in.

Something new and wonderful awaits me! The future.

FU-TU-RE. I want the future. I dread the future. What is the future? Is it something people can feel? Or sense? How does the future work? The future is in diaries. It is squares of blank time that you fill in with appointments and events. I want to fill my diary with:

♥ SATURDAY 10TH JUNE

3.00pm Lynx and M get married!

♥ MONDAY 25TH SEPTEMBER

Lynx and M buy a three-bedroomed house in Raleigh Drive.

My future!

And here I am waiting at the agreed meeting point. I am wearing a pink Coca-Cola t-shirt, black leggings, pink and white checked Vans, a small square purple and pink bag across my shoulder, a little purple flower in my hair and smoky eyes! I know I look good, so why don't I feel confident?

I wait.

Date Mask fully on.

Other people are waiting too. Checking their phones. I check mine. Text from Mum.

> You all right Baby? Shall I collect you later?? Xxxxx :-)

I text back:

> Fine. No.

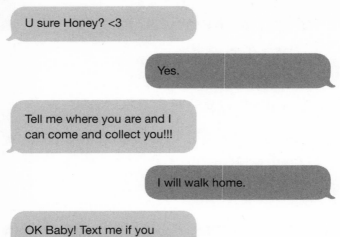

U sure Honey? <3

Yes.

Tell me where you are and I can come and collect you!!!

I will walk home.

OK Baby! Text me if you change your mind M XXXX

She always complains my texts are too short, but I think her texts are too long and I don't need her smiley faces and hearts right now. I am trying to grow up. Grow away. Get a hunky boyfriend...work towards dinner under the stars on a beach in Cephalonia!

I go to the film poster and check the time: 6.15.

5.30.

They will be here in 15 minutes. So we have half an hour to do:

Small talk. (And I've practised this using Skylar's Dating Tips webpage. "Hey! Really excited about this movie!

It's got super cool reviews and it's on my must-see list!
What other movies are you guys interested in seeing?")

Buy ticket.

Pick and mix – pink marshmallows, white
chocolate mice and strawberry bon bons (will all
look fab with my outfit and create a great sense of
satisfying co-ordination for me).

The schedule is tight but we can all be seated
by 6.15 as the adverts begin for the film! I clap my
hands and then squeeze them by my sides as I see
Shaznia and Jake walk towards me. Shaznia waves! I
wave back. She is wearing what I suggested. Slouchy
jeans, pink Vans, black and white t-shirt and the
tailored jacket I lent her. Plus she uses delicate gold
(fake) jewellery as a feature and she's got smoky eyes.
I go to tell her she looks great but she gets in first:

"Lynx is going to be late."

L

A

T

E

I feel like I am hanging in the January air.

Anxiety appears. Right in my face. Its opportunity here.

LATE!!!!!!!? Date Mask slips and I go bright, bright red, **BURNING** and juddering.

"How late?" I ask. She checks her phone. I can see Jake in my peripheral vision but I can't look at him. I don't want him here. I don't know Jake.

"Errr…" She looks through her texts. "Errr…" She keeps scrolling. "Ermm."

"Well, when did he text you?!" And then Jake adds, "About five minutes ago."

"Well, why are you taking so long to find the text Shaznia?"

"All right M, don't shout!"

"Sorry, sorry," I say. I didn't realise I was shouting, and then she reads it. I try to secure my slipped mask but it's so hard. Am I still shouting? I don't mean to shout. I take a deep breath. She reads,

"Sorry. Gonna be 20–30 mins late."

And this means NO PICK AND MIX. NO PREPARED CHATTING. NO TICKETS??? WILL WE EVEN GET TO THE FILM ON TIME?????????????

Anxiety's gnarly, powerful hands are gripping my shoulders and I can hear its heavy breathing in my ears. It **kicks** the back of my knees and my legs W-O-B-B-L-e.

"Let's go in and get the tickets?" suggests Jake.

Everything is scrambled.

"Don't worry M!" says Shaznia. "It's not like you've been stood up!"

Stood up? I am standing up, well, trying, my legs are shaking so badly. And I want to ask what she means – "stood up." But I can't, and I can feel the nerves around my eyes twitching and I can't control them. No control of the little nerves around my eyes and no control of my life.

20–30 minutes?

They go in and buy tickets and I wait. Wait. Waiting for how long? 20–30 minutes. Does that mean 25 minutes? And I look at my phone. So, he should be here between 6.20 and 6.30.

I could just bolt home. BOLT. I could just go into MOLW and find sanctuary by a lake and a view of the mountains, but this is a date with Lynx!

I take a deep breath.

But Anxiety doesn't back off.

People hanging around, looking at me… Cars are roaring past. Sirens are screaming. Sirens are never good. Sirens always mean bad is happening. Texts are bleeping, and I look up at the sky and I am so grateful for the grey sky keeping a lid on my emotions, because if it wasn't for the clouds above I would be a volcano. Mount Etna! Lava and hot! HoT! Molten ash exploding out of me.

"Got your ticket hun." Shaznia and Jake return.

"Thank you." I take the ticket and feel relieved that I have something to hold.

"Careful M, you'll rip it!" she says. Then she and Jake stand *really* close to each other and she giggles a lot. STANDING CLOSE. I don't want to stand that close to anyone. Even Lynx. I look down the road and think I could bolt down there. Bolt down that road and get back to my little, pink bedroom, and I know Anxiety will chase me, but maybe I could escape it or deal with it on my own, not with Shaznia and Jake and Lynx!

But as I look down the road I see Lynx, walking towards us.

Juicy kissable lips, sensitive sparkling eyes, soft glowing skin and a cool, calm aura.

And I swear the sun cracks through the grey clouds, just a little, and lights up a path for him as he strides towards me.

His blue chambray shirt and jeans is way more sophisticated than a boy from Sevenoaks should be and I know that's partly why I love him so much because he has style equal to mine. We are both trapped in this suburban world of track suits and together we transcend it! He should be on the pages of a magazine or modelling on a cat walk in Paris.

We would look amazing together and mini explosions fire off all round my head and my body and I am electric! I feel like I've been plugged in!

But he's late.

Suddenly he's arrived! He's in our group zone. This moment that I have been dreaming of! Imagining!!! It is here! The four of us are standing together and he says to me,

"Hi M, you look nice." And I reply,

"You're late!"

Shaznia gasps. Jake looks at his trainers.

"Hello would have been nice," says Lynx.

The volcano is rumbling. I'm not sure the January sky can keep a lid on my emotions…

"Being on time would have been nice. Why are you late?" I ask.

"I'm sorry, it was the traffic, and there was an accident. I thought you guys would have heard all the sirens. So my dad had to drop me off on the other side of town."

"But why didn't you plan for an accident and allow time, so that being late wouldn't happen?" And Shaznia says,

"OMG, M! He was only half an hour late. It wasn't his fault!"

And I know she is right. I know that I should hold back but I can't. I am off. Loose. I need to say what's in me.

"It may have only been half an hour for you but for me it felt like an eternity."

"Oh, I didn't realise me and Jake's company was that bad M?"

"No! No! That's not what I mean." And Jake continues to look at his shoes.

"Look. Why don't we go in?" says Lynx. "It doesn't matter if we miss the start because I've seen it, so I can fill you in on what happens."

And that just feels so selfish. He's seen it. So he's OK and doesn't seem to care that we will miss the beginning. The order of the story. So I tell him,

"That's just selfish! Leaving us out here and you've seen it anyway!"

"M, relax!" shouts Shaznia.

"Do you know what?" says Lynx. "Shaznia was right. You are the weird one."

THE VOLCANO EXPLODES.

"WEIRD?????"

Jake walks off.

"I am very concerned about this date," I declare. My voice is shaking and tears are preparing to drop, heavily.

"What date? Who said this was a date?" asks Lynx.

Shaznia walks off after Jake.

"This date. The one we planned."

"What? Is this a date?"

"Yes. It was. WAS. This date is now officially not a date."

And I bolt. I bolt down the street and disappear away. Far, far away from this horrible, cruel situation and all these bad words and confusing tones and messed-up times that I just don't understand. Lynx and M buy a three-bedroomed house in Raleigh Drive seems very unlikely right now.

And of course Anxiety is racing after me as I run home, and of course it's pacing beside me now, jeering at me, trying to trip me up so I'll stop and freeze in the street, but I keep running.

Past The Money Shop and I can just about see the M through the haze of pink mist in MOLW. MY safe, beautiful, uneventful little world of mountain streams and delicate flowers. On my own without any complications. I don't need any one. I don't want anything, just to be left alone. Because my world is good but I wanted a beach dinner under the stars in Cephalonia. Wouldn't any girl?

"Shaznia was right, you are weird! Shaznia was right, you are weird! Shaznia was right, you are weird!"

When did she say this? At the New Year's Eve party I was not invited to? Weird. Weird. Why am I weird? Is it really weird to be on time?

And I can't think of anywhere in the *Cherry Magazine* Friendship Special where it says it is acceptable for a friend to call you weird behind your back. What she has done is very, very wrong and betrayal lodges in my gut, heavy and SOUR.

Please don't use my weaknesses against me.

★ Chapter 11 ★

And I've been fighting autism. I thought I could pretend I didn't have it!

I truly believed that if I followed the instructions in all the magazines and websites and if I copied Skylar I could trick autism and make it go away. I could hide from it, throw it aside, but no it doesn't work like that. I'm stuck with it. All the rules that work for everyone else, all the normal girls, don't apply to me. So what, what am I supposed to do now? Where do I turn? Who do I turn to?

Sour, sour, sour. Bitter. Bile in my mouth. Betrayal.

Monday morning arrives and I am heavy with dread. I lie in bed with no idea on how I am going to get through the day...let alone the week...the year.

Time and problems  up against me.

All weekend Mum kept knocking at my door, sitting on the edge of my bed and asking questions.

Knock Knock Knock Knock Knock Knock Knock Knock Knock Knock Knock Knock Knock Knock

"M, please, darling. What happened?

Have you had a fight with Shaznia?

Was Joe there?

I didn't think you liked cinemas?

You weren't out that long?

Did Shaznia say something horrible to you M?"

Again and again she asks.

But I wouldn't tell her. I couldn't tell her. I couldn't talk and get the words out about the betrayal, and now it's Monday morning and I just want to stay in my little bed, wrapped up in my purple and grey blanket, and I've decided I think I should avoid words and speaking because it gets me in trouble and causes me so many terrible, terrible problems. I get words and their meanings wrong and I don't understand the language people are using.

"Come on M. Come on! It's 8.00. You're going to be late for school!" But I can't get up. "I'm so worried about you M!" And I think, so am I, Mum, so am I. She sits down on the edge of my bed. "Please M. Please, tell me what happened on Saturday."

M SILENCE

"Did something *awful* happen?"

And I nod. And Mum stands up and repeats,

"Oh my god, oh my god, oh my god! Did someone touch you? Has someone attacked you?"

And I shake my head and think how Anxiety attacks all the time…but I know that's not what she means. She kneels beside the bed. Her eyes are very sharp and the lines on her forehead are very deep. She gets close to my face and looks deep into my eyes. She is examining my face. I turn my face into the pillow and pull the blanket around me – TIGHTER. Her voice is low. What does that mean???

"Well what M? Please help me here. Do I need to call the police?"

I shake my head and I hear her let out a big breath of air.

"Was it an argument?"

And I just don't want to relive this ordeal.

"A disagreement?"

I nod.

"Just a disagreement."

Just?

"With Shaznia?"

And I nod again and I can tell she is crying. Why is she crying? Why does my sadness make her cry? Even when I don't talk it causes problems! What am I to do!?? I lift my head from the pillow and I want to reach out to her and touch her, but she might take it the wrong way! I don't want to upset her more.

"I'm so sorry M, but I'm just so pleased that nothing awful has happened and that some terrible person…did do something terrible to you."

But I think they did.

And I watch Mum's teary face as she says she never liked Shaznia and that if "whatever has happened" means I spend less time with Shaznia then this could be a positive thing. But I fail to see that this is positive.

This just isn't the case. She stands up. She takes my uniform out of the wardrobe.

"M, you have to go to school and I need to get to work. I can't be late either."

I don't move.

"I know it might be a difficult day but you will have to go and face her at some point. Everyone has disagreements with friends…or people at school or work, and we can't hide away from them. I'm afraid it's life."

I shake my head.

"M, it's the law. Legally you have to go to school, and if you don't I could get in a lot of trouble."

Sirens screech in my head.

"There was that story in the paper about that mum who had to go to prison because she couldn't get her daughter to school."

The sirens are louder.

Mum places my shiny, black ballet pumps by my bed.

"You *have* to go to school."

I get up, put my uniform on, my shiny shoes and NO FACE. I go to school…

★ ★ ★

I enter my form room and see a girl on the other side of the room and I wonder who it is. She looks exhausted. Is that a new girl? And then I realise it's me. It's my reflection in the window. I hardly recognise myself. All I've done is lie on my bed since Saturday. I didn't leave the room but my head was everywhere. Racing and dashing from one thought to another.

I have to walk past Shaznia's desk to get to mine. She's in a huddle with Nev and Lara. All I can see is shoulders and their backs with low murmurs rising from them. I can't make out any words, but whatever they are I don't think they're complimentary. Then Shaznia raises her head from the huddle and says,

"Hi M."

But I don't answer. I don't want to talk any more.

"Rude," Lara calls out.

The jacket I lent Shaznia is thrown over my desk. My beautiful jacket all creased and uncared for. I run my hand over the material and try to smooth it out and I can smell her on it. Her stain on my jacket, and I know I can't wear it again.

I sit down next to Joe and he asks me lots of questions but I don't know the answers. I don't know any more. I'm not sure I ever knew, but I can't pretend today. Today I am wearing NO FACE. She is my mask.

I WEAR HER WHEN I FEEL POINTLESS.

I can't see the point in me and how I fit into all this: school, family, people. And I look out the window and I see all the trees. They calm me, and I know I fit in with the trees and the sky and I wonder if anyone sees the trees the way I do…and I realise that of course they don't. No one sees anything the way I do. They hear different. See different. Smell different. Taste different. So I have to live in this world on my own and I can't fit in this world. We share this world, but I seem to be the one doing all the sharing. Constantly. The hard bit.

Mr Bray enters the class room and shouts,
"QUIET EVERYONE!"

But I can still hear murmurs.

And I attempt to work through the timetables of time, labelled Monday.

MONDAY	TUESDAY	WEDNESDAY	THURSDAY	FRIDAY
Maths	Geography	English	French	Art
Art	Maths	English	PSE	Art
Science	French	RE	Geography	PSE
Science	RE	Maths	Maths	French
LUNCH LUNCH LUNCH				
History	English	PE	English	PSE
French	PSE	History	English	Drama

I stand in the doorway of the maths corridor. On the edge. To walk down it would be foolish. The fear of Mrs Chiswick telling me off for not attending the lesson isn't as bad as the corridor noises that will pierce my brain and rip at my skin and add to the pressure in my head.

Anxiety has been following me around but gets a great opportunity to kick me, hard, in the back of my knees again. My legs W-O-B-B-L-e.

Students brush and bash past me. Lara's bag **HITS** my left arm.

"Careful M!" she says.

I grab my arm. Owww.

"Don't be late M," says Nev, "I've heard being on time is *very* important for you." Nev and Lara laugh. They huddle together and stroll, effortlessly, up the corridor.

She knows. They know. They know everything.

And now gossip and Saturday night's events are loose! Zig-zagging round all the corridors in the school!

Anxiety looms over me. It's much, much bigger than me today. Wider. Taller. Stronger. I don't think I can take it on today.

Joe appears by my side. My arm aches.

"I'll walk with you." I shake my head. I can't walk up that corridor. Anxiety will launch a full-on assault.

And I see a poster on a notice board. A helpline number, but who do I call for help? Who can possibly help me with this?

"M, I have to go to Maths." And he walks up the corridor…just like that.

And there's a bench outside, by the main entrance, so I go there. Sit there for a while on my own.

To breathe and try to keep anxiety at a distance. Like what Fiona says, taking some time out. "To breathe and create some physical and mental space from your problem."

And then a problem arrives at the bench.

"M, do you know where you need to be right now?" Head of Pastoral Care Miss Twinnings sits next to me. "It's Maths, isn't it, M?" And she's totally wrong. This is where I need to be right now.

"It's January M and it is not an appropriate time to sit on a bench outside." And I think to myself how this is the best time of year to sit on a bench. No one else is about. And I hear her say a mixture of things. A muddle of threats.

REPORT CARD

HEAD'S OFFICE

MAKE THE RIGHT CHOICE OR

CODE OF CONDUCT

And I watch a blackbird hopping about on the grass.

"M! Are you listening?" Miss Twinnings shouts, and I watch the bird fly off. Lucky bird. Just leaving when he wants. Not trapped. "Look, M, I know your mum asked us to send that email round about the… autism…and I've got to be honest I'm not keen on labels, but I've done the autism awareness course last year, so I know what's going on here, and you are probably waiting for some very straightforward instructions, aren't you?"

She's saying autism with gaps on either side of the word. Why? Is she uncomfortable with autism? I am, and her gaps around the word don't help and don't make me feel good. Is she afraid of saying autism? Then she instructs me,

"Stand up."

But why? Why would I stand up? I have made the right choice. If I stand up I worry that will be the wrong choice, but I need to be on my own, so I do stand up…

"Well done, M. That is the *right* choice."

…and I walk over to another bench by the French Block. I want to be on my own. I know that is the *right* choice. She follows me.

"That is rude behaviour M. You are not following instructions and are being blatantly rude. You are causing unnecessary trouble."

But I'm not causing trouble! She's the one causing trouble. I just want to be left alone. Is that so wrong? I look down at my patent, black ballet shoes.

"It's my job to make sure you attend your lessons," she shouts.

And I think she's not very good at her job, and I turn away from her because her shouting pierces at my brain.

"Right, that's it. First walking away from me and now turning your back on a member of staff is unacceptable. You are automatically on a Section 2 of the St. Andrew's Disciplinary Code of Conduct." And a Code of Conduct does sound very BIG and important, and then she sits down beside me. I continue to look at my shiny shoes.

"This is all very serious M." Does she know about Saturday and Lynx and Shaznia? The gossip has been released around the school like an uncontrollable virus in a film! And I can't stop it! And now even Miss Twinnings knows about the betrayal and she probably thinks I'm really stupid too.

"Can we do a deal M?"

And I think about Lynx...and how I have ruined everything. How I wish I really understood how I could get it all so very wrong.

Last Saturday before 4.45 life was so very different. So much less complicated and difficult... How I long for it to be Saturday 4.44 and I could have another chance.

"M, if you go to your next lesson, I could see past all this and I won't put you on the **CODE OF CONDUCT** and we won't have to fill in all the forms and stay late after school...eh?"

...I'll never have a Card Emporium series of life events, filled with lots of sparkly cards celebrating all these big life events. I was on course and now I'm not. I skidded off. Badly.

And the bell rings for the next lesson. So I get up, as I can't get any time on my own and I need to be on my own.

"Well done M, and you know you can talk to me about any worries whenever you need. I am available any time between 1 and 2 Tuesday to Thursday" – and I think how I wish my worries were only between 1 and 2 Tuesdays to Thursdays...not constant, and I bolt home.

★ ★ ★

"I think she just needed some time out." Mum is sitting on the edge of my bed. She is still in her coat. Miss Twinnings called her at work and she rushed home and now Mum is talking to her on the speaker phone. We are having an "inclusion call." I am curled up under my purple and grey blanket. It is 11.15 and I should be in Science, not on an inclusion call.

"And remember the email you sent out about M's...autism...and –" Miss Twinnings doesn't let my mum finish.

"She needs to come into school tomorrow morning."

"I KNOW she needs to go to school tomorrow morning but I am concerned it won't be that straightforward." But Miss Twinnings doesn't listen.

"Lack of attendance doesn't do the student or school any favours and results in low grades."

"OK, OK. I agree…but is there something we can do to make it easier for M?"

"Does your husband have any influence over M?" Mum stands up and her voice goes low. Why does it go low?

"No, he's…not here… We're separated."

"Well, perhaps that's why she's so upset?"

Mum is now pacing round and round my little room and Anxiety is outside on the landing.

"He is present in our family life and it is not relevant." Mum's words are sharp and tight. Is she angry with Miss Twinnings, like she gets with me? And then Mum opens the door and walks out onto the landing and she lets Anxiety in, and it's not an "inclusion call" any more because I can't hear Miss Twinnings, only my mum saying,

"Yes…" and "I agree but M isn't…" and "OK. OK…yes…"

And what are they saying? What are they planning?

Mum re-enters, clicks the phone off, and throws it on my bed and shouts at it,

"Incompetent *bloody* woman…!" She puts her face in her hands and shakes her head. "Miss Twinnings says you can work in the library tomorrow and she'll come and meet you after lunch. You won't have to see any of those girls or walk down the maths corridor or any of the other bloody corridors."

And she can't promise I won't see Shaznia or Nev or Lara. She just can't.

Anxiety sits on the edge of my bed. Staring at me.

Autism is an invisible cloak of chains, ropes and weights.

★ Chapter 12 ★

It's Tuesday 8.15am. I am curled up in my blanket. Very tightly. Mum is sitting on the edge of my bed. She is now talking to Dad on speaker phone.

"I can't force her to go in, Simon. I can't physically dress a 13-year-old girl and take her into the school, can I? You need to tell her, Simon. Tell her to get up and go to school."

"M. You need to get up and go to school." Dad's voice and instructions through the phone feel weird and odd. Disconcerting.

"Tell her, tell her it's the law and she has to go to school." And Dad repeats this,

"It's the law M and you have to go to school."

Sirens go off in my head and I screw into a tighter little ball. Dad continues, "Come on M. We can't just take a day off when we fancy it…because something difficult has happened. Sometimes we have to soldier on."

"Do you not think I have told her that, Simon? To be honest, I don't know why I bothered ringing you."

"I'm trying here, Mandy."

"You should try getting her up one morning."

"Yeah but it's a bit difficult because if you recall, Mandy, you kicked me out."

Mum turns the phone off and throws it on the bed. "He makes me so bloody angry!" And then she throws her anger at me.

"M, get up. I have to go to work. I cannot take a day off. We've got designers coming in to the studio in less than one hour and I need to get there! I NEED you to get up!"

I am so tired and I couldn't sleep last night because I have been worrying about Nev and Lara and Shaznia and all the gossip going round and round the corridors and classrooms. All night Anxiety, pacing around my room, my little pink room. Relentless. Exhausting.

And I know Mum said I won't see "those girls," but she can't promise. She just can't.

"It's the law, M, they'll send me to prison if you don't get up for school!"

Sirens screech and big sets of prison keys jangle round my head. I get up, in the hope the sirens and jangles will stop! And I wonder do other people go to school because they are scared of their mums going to prison or...or just because they'd like to learn?

Fluffy animals are singing in my head and the mad Hatter's having a tea party, so sorry I can't concentrate.

★ Chapter 13 ★

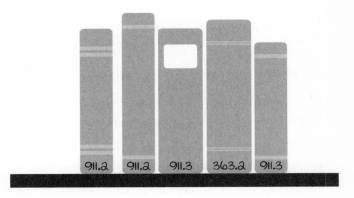

911.2   911.2   911.3   363.2   911.3

I like the order of books and the numbers on the spines. Each number relates to a subject. And I feel as though these numbers, this system, is kind to me and how I feel. Kind numbers. It's a room, a world that caters for me and how I feel. Straightforward and clear. It doesn't hide information. It helps me *find* information, so I can learn and fit in. I feel safe in the library.

I sit at a desk. Waiting for Miss Twinnings. She said she would meet me here after lunch.

I see a book in the wrong order and I feel disordered inside. Something is not as it should be.

I re-shelve it, to its correct position. It feels like the whole room relaxes and is re-set. The librarian looks up.

"Thank you," she whispers.

I like the library but this is not where I should be. I should be in Geography. I was late for school, and as Mum kept reminding me in the car it was my fault and my decision to be late by staying in bed, but it isn't really my fault. Autism has dictated all this and I did NOT choose to have autism.

The library is quiet most of the time, and throughout the morning it was mostly me and a Year 8, with period pain, who sat on one of the comfy chairs with a hot water bottle.

Miss Twinnings said she would be here after lunch. So I am sitting here waiting for "after lunch."

I catch myself tapping my cheeks. I sit on my hands.

Mum called Miss Twinnings incompetent this morning but I don't know what that means. Maybe it's an illness or a religion. I see a dictionary in the reference section and look up INCOMPETENT.

Incompetent

[adjective]

Not possessing the necessary ability, skill to do or carry out a task; incapable of carrying out one's job effectively. Marked by lack of ability, skill, etc.

The bell rings for break.

The library door opens and Joe appears by my desk.

"This is rubbish M. Mr Bray said in registration that you're working in the library. I can't believe you have to sit here. Shouldn't it be Shaznia in here? What've you done wrong?"

"I think it's because I ran off from Miss Twinnings... And other stuff."

"Running off from her is called self-survival... She'd send armies of grown men crying back to their mothers...joke...kind of... I could call over this evening and bring you the homework?"

I shake my head.

"Do you want *anything*?"

I shake my head.

"Here." He hands me a Twix from his blazer pocket and I think how this is the nicest thing that's happened to me for...for so long.

"Thanks," I whisper.

The bell rings.

"I'll text you later."

And I wanted to ask him all about Shaznia, has she said anything else about me? And has Lara said anything or Nev? But I don't want to know, but I do want to know. What are they saying about me?

"Here." The librarian is now standing by me. She places two books on the desk. "This is about space." She flips through beautiful pages of colourful planets. Full of facts and figures, and charts. "And this a poetry book," she says. "You're Year 8, aren't you?"

I nod.

"And you're meant to be in English, aren't you?"

I look at the carpet, ashamed of why I'm not.

"Well this poetry book might help with English, plus it's my favourite book in the whole library. Maybe you'll enjoy it too." And she returns to her desk.

I look through the books and check, check, check, check, check, check the library clock. Waiting for "after lunch."

The library is busy with students throughout lunch and my safe haven has been invaded by these book-borrowing annoyances.

1.50.

The bell ri**ngs** again and the library empties.

"Miss Twinnings did say she'd be here after lunch, didn't she?" asks the librarian.

I nod, but I wonder WHEN after lunch? Lunch at St. Andrew's ends at officially 1.50. A bell rings out all across the whole school. You can't avoid it! I wish I could avoid the bell. I can't hide from its harshness. It is very clear that lunch ends at 1.50. I pull – pull – pull on my fingers and my knuckles click and I think about why I am here, in exile.

Lynx Lynx Lynx Lynx Lynx Lynx Lynx Lynx
Lynx Lynx Lynx Lynx Lynx Lynx Lynx Lynx
Lynx Lynx Lynx

"Miss Twinnings often runs late," she says. "You're the girl in the school with autism, aren't you? Miss Twinnings sent the email out?"

I nod, but I can't be the only one. I read on a website that 1 in 83 people are on the autistic spectrum, so that must mean there are 23 people at St. Andrew's like me. I calculate that there are 72 staff (including full and part-time), so there is a high probability that one member of staff is too. And I wonder about Mr Crane, but he's not like me at all.

I really am very alone with this.

"Between you and me, M, it really annoys me that she said 'after lunch.' It's very irritating."

I look into her eyes. Briefly.

"It's inconsiderate," she adds.

Does she know how I feel?

I flip through the pages of the poetry book and momentarily my mind is taken away from the time. There is a chapter called "Love Poems" and I read the first line of a poem called "i carry your heart with me." And I understand that the poet just can't stop thinking about the person he loves… The person he loves has become part of him.

i carry your heart with me(i carry it in

my heart),i am never without it

> Lynx Lynx Lynx Lynx Lynx Lynx Lynx Lynx Lynx Lynx Lynx Lynx Lynx Lynx Lynx Lynx Lynx Lynx Lynx

2.50. I want to get home and watch Skylar on YouTube but I am beginning to feel angry at Skylar and her perfect world and how all the boys really fancy her, but I can't go straight home because it is Tuesday so I am going to see Fiona, and I don't want to see Fiona but I do want to see Fiona. Where will I begin?

"Shaznia was right, you are weird! Shaznia was right, you are weird! Shaznia was right, you are weird!"

And I breathe deeply and the ticking clock gets louder and louder and I replay Saturday again and again. Why did I say such stupid things?

Anxiety appears from behind a book shelf and lurches towards me.

I take a deep breath and it backs off.

And the girl with the period pain goes back to class and a boy from Year 11 limps in and now he sits in the comfy chair. The sick chair. I'm not sick. I'm not ill. Why have I been put in the library?

I look through the big, shiny book called *Our Solar System* and read that Earth is the fifth biggest planet in the solar system, with a diameter of 8000 miles, that it's 4.5 billion years old and spins on its axis every 23 hours and 56 minutes and has a liquid metal inner core that's hotter than the surface of the sun.

The Earth is so vast! So deep! So fast! And here I am sat on a grey plastic chair in a library, in a school that stinks of disinfectant and sweat, and I think surely there must be somewhere else for me? Somewhere on this massive planet where I won't be punished or exiled for being me?

It is 3.15 and Miss Twinnings crashes through the door carrying a mug of coffee and a pile of folders.

"Sorry! Sorry! Sorry! Hello Julia," she says to the librarian. "Very busy day!" She spots me and says, "I'm so sorry M. I've had a Year 9 with an asthma attack and I've had all this urgent paper work, but I'll meet you in here first thing tomorrow morning. OK?"

First thing?

The bell **rings.**

"Is that OK M?" I stare at the carpet. I am trying to let the ringing pass through my body.

"M, is there anything you need to say before I go to my next meeting?" and I nod.

"I've got back-to-back meetings till 6.00, so you need to tell me ASAP. You know you can say anything to me M. I'm not here to judge." So I tell her,

"Mum's right, you are incompetent."

I see the librarian laughing and Miss Twinnings turns red. Her voice is much louder and she says, "Tomorrow. First thing M," and crashes back out the library.

★ ★ ★

I am in the reception of:

Good Life

Therapy Centre

A place to thrive and
reach your full potential

Fiona Lacy, PhD, LLC
Child & Adolescent Psychological Services

I am 10 minutes early and sit in the waiting room.

I don't really want to talk.

The school gates are **CLANGING** in my head.

Debbie, the Head's PA, shouted at me,

"Don't run!"

Her words bat about inside my skull.

Maybe Fiona would understand if I didn't talk today. I want to keep sealed up. Perhaps I could say a few words?

The waiting room clock ticks its way to 4.00 and then wonderfully, beautifully soft, reassuringly honest Fiona opens the door to the safe powder blue room.

"Hello M. Do come in," says Fiona.

We sit. She smiles. I copy her and smile.

COUNSELLOR SILENCE

And she says,

"M, I have some news for you."

NOT "Tell me about your week M." Fiona should say "Tell me about your week M."

COUNSELLOR SILENCE

This was odd. This is wrong. When I enter the room and sit in my comfy beige chair Fiona should say *"Tell me about your week M."* And then I tell her.

And the powder blue room is one of the only places I really talk as it's a safe space. Fiona has made it a safe place…until she said:

"M, I have some news for you."

And she tells me her news.

"I am having a baby and will be leaving to go on maternity leave, in three months."

And the powder blue room becomes as dangerous as everywhere else in the world.

"I know more than anyone how **CHANGE** is difficult for you M and…" The word *change* **JARS** in my head and creates an *INTERFERENCE* so I can't really hear Fiona's words.

CH and the AN and GE clanged and stuck and jarred in my thought processes. Jarred.

"M, how is this making you feel?" she asks.

I say nothing.

"I think you look a little…uncomfortable M."

COUNSELLOR SILENCE

Clanging and jarring and interference is uncomfortable and I start to think about MOLW – My Own Little World. I look up at the three smooth pebbles by the still lake and the word Tranquil.

It's very like MOLW. Where I take myself off sometimes. My world doesn't have smooth pebbles lined up by the edge of still water but it does have a pink mountain range with cool, clear water trickling down the sides to a stream, surrounded by a safe forest and a gentle sun, glowing in the pale blue sky, and I drift into MOLW. My safe place…and then I hear Fiona say,

"It's a lovely picture, isn't it M?"

I look at the beige carpet. The three stains since my first session, all that time ago, are still there.

"Tranquillity is a lovely feeling, isn't it M?"

I can't talk to Fiona any more.

"How are *you* feeling M? How are you feeling right now?"

COUNSELLOR SILENCE

"Goodbyes and endings can be very difficult M. It's very common to feel, well…lost or sad or angry."

I feel lots of things and, yes, anger is one of those feelings.

I loved the pattern of Tuesdays at 4.00 and knowing the appointment hung, beautifully, in that time. A solid time with a clock in the room so I could watch the hands move and see what portion of time I had left. My safe space, but an epic change, the size of the iceberg that destroyed the Titanic, has hit me. I've been thrown out into the cold, dark sea and she talks about how she will be back in about a year.

A year, out here on my own?

A YEAR????

"M, is that clear? I will repeat all the information again M and I can write it down too." But I heard the key words:

Leaving

Baby

Maternity leave

"So there is lots of time to put plans in place and to meet up with someone who specialises in adolescent counselling."

ANOTHER counsellor? Fiona is *my* counsellor, and now some stupid baby is going to get in the way, and I think about how I've come here today, to try and talk about Lynx and the date and Shaznia and now *this* has happened.

This break of agreement.

Our 50 minutes is over, she stands up and I can see her belly is rounder and she is pregnant, and she must have been sitting there for months knowing she was going to leave and have a baby. Letting me talk and share all my feelings and all the time she knew she was leaving. She opens the door, and as usual Mum is waiting for me and again something different happens. Fiona talks.

"So M, I've given your mum a list of counsellors who I think you would work well with, and I suggest you start calling them or visiting them."

"Thank you Fiona," says Mum. "That sounds like a great idea, doesn't it M?"

And as we walk towards the car, Mum says,

"We'll call some of these numbers tomorrow M and find you another counsellor. Fiona said it's important you continue with this process."

Had they been talking? When did Fiona say this?

"Fiona said that it's OK if you feel you need a few weeks off talking to someone. She said it would give you time to reflect but that it's good to get some structured emotional support back in your life soon."

Reflect? On Fiona's betrayal.

"And Fiona says to always remember it's a good technique to write down how you feel and get your feelings 'out there in the world!'"

I look at Mum. I am furious.

"Ermmm, am I not being clear? 'Out there in the world'…well… It means express yourself while letting go of feelings. 'Letting them out into the world.'"

Sometimes life just gets more and more ridiculous.

I do like the idea of not feeling furious. I'd much rather be tranquil, but how do you let your feelings out into the world? Is it like letting Bella out into the back garden? I haven't got a back door. I can't just open a door to me and let my feelings out into the world. Is that what everyone else is doing? Am I surrounded by other people's feelings that they've let out?? Do I pick them up as I pass someone in town or do other people's anger or jealousy latch on to me as I walk down a corridor? And is that why I get so anxious? I've picked up all the dumped emotions everyone else has let out into the world and I have an extra quota of feelings? I would like to release all these emotions but I can't. I am stuck with being furious.

We're in the car now and I'm still listening to Mum.

"And Grandma said she'd continue paying for the sessions. So there is no need for you or us to worry about money."

So Grandma's in on the big betrayal too, huh? Grandma, Mum, Fiona, who else is on the list of people who've been talking about me and my confidential process? Who else, eh????? And then she adds,

"Even your dad thinks it's a good idea and he's not one to believe in counselling and therapies."

Dad????? I make a note to be careful what information I tell these four in future.

"You know you can tell me what you say in the sessions with Fiona… As your mother, maybe I should know?"

SILENCE as we pass The Money Shop and a poster advertising organic Milk.

"It's difficult to know what you are thinking M. What are you thinking? Are you thinking about the new counsellor?"

What I'm thinking is, I wonder will we pass Lynx in the car?

People say I keep choosing the wrong times to do things but autism is very inconvenient.

★ Chapter 14 ★

"I'll give her a call," says the librarian and she dials Miss Twinnings' extension number. Voice mail.

I should be in Geography. Geography doing "Global Hazards." And I think I am one big global hazard to myself.

"Hi Miss Twinnings, it's Julia from the library. It's 9.46am and you were meant to be meeting M from 8b first thing. She is waiting for you." She puts the receiver down.

"Have you got any work to do?" she asks. I reach into my bag and take out my geography book.

"It's not fair, all this, is it M?" and she sits opposite me. "When you're on the spectrum you could do without all this stress, couldn't you? I mean Miss Twinnings being late. Being vague is really stressful."

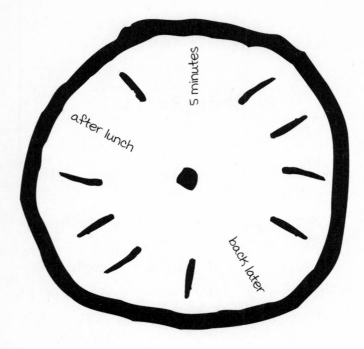

"They don't do clocks with 'after lunch' and 'first thing' do they? It's irritating." I look at her, briefly. "She says she'll do one thing, then does another. How are you supposed to get on with your day when she totally disrupts it?"

She understands.

She hands me a school laptop.

"Here, you can download all the worksheets for your classes and the lesson outlines. Try and keep up with your work. It would be a shame to fall behind in your lessons, wouldn't it?"

I nod, but to be honest it's all chaotic in my head. I'm not sure where I am in my lessons.

"I'll ring Miss Twinnings again and remind her you are here."

I try to find the file marked Geography and lots of sub-folders flash up.

Global hazards. Surge storms 1953. Tsunamis.

Avalanches. Struggling earth.

What will the world be like in 2030?

2030? I just want to make it to lunch time, never mind 2030. Overwhelming!

The library door opens and I look up, expecting Miss Twinnings, but it's a teaching assistant with a sobbing girl from Year 9. The librarian and the TA settle her and bring her water and tissues. Anyone could come in here. What if Shaznia wants to borrow a book? Or Nev or Lara? Anxiety hits my head and sends a jolt of fear through me like an electric shock. But Lynx could come to the library! What if Lynx comes and wants to take a book out?

Lynx Lynx Lynx Lynx Lynx Lynx Lynx Lynx
Lynx Lynx Lynx Lynx Lynx Lynx Lynx Lynx
Lynx Lynx

I Google the school football team and I look at the pictures of Lynx and his eyes and the deep regret I have for messing things up with him. If I didn't care about being late and I hadn't been so very, very stressed I might be his girlfriend now. Maybe I still could be? Maybe there is a way of making it all better? I had this golden opportunity to be in his company and I ruined it. RUINED IT. I shouldn't have got so angry and I replay it again and again in my head. How come Shaznia and Jake didn't care that he was late?

I find more photos of Lynx on an adventure weekend in North Wales and he's standing on the mountain and the caption says, *"On Top of the World! We did it!"*

I look at Facebook and Shaznia has added more of him at the New Year's Eve party. The party I wasn't invited to, but that must have been the party he asked about me and they arranged the date, and suddenly these pictures seem really important. My name must have been at this party.

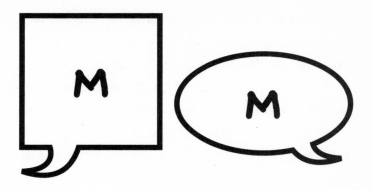

My name was uttered and I was spoken of for being wanted and pretty by Lynx! So I copy these pictures onto a document and I call the document "Date Beginnings." And there are five photos of Lynx at this party.

Lynx holding up a drink.

Lynx in a selfie with Jake.

Lynx with his arm around Shaznia's shoulders.

Lynx smiling. A big, juicy-lipped, sparkly smile.

Lynx with a group of Year 10s.

I then create a file called "Lynx Love <3" and save all these pictures to email to myself on my laptop at home. It's like the beginning of our story.

I gaze at him. His smile. His sparkly eyes. His long-legged, lanky kindness and gelled hair. I fill more pages with these pictures, 20 pictures on each page, and I create more pages, and I don't intend to print them off, just keep them, locked in my laptop. Keeping him close to me. The library phone rings and cuts through the library quiet. The librarian answers,

"Well, can you give me an exact time Miss Twinnings? I know… I know you are busy but I think she'd appreciate a time… OK… OK."

She puts the receiver down and walks over to me.

"She'll be here after lunch."

I look at the clock. It's 11.15.

I should be in English now and I think of the peeling paint in English Room B15 and tap my face. I think of how we are reading Jane Eyre today and that woman who is locked in the attic and I think that's like me, except I've been put away in the library, out of sight, because no one knows what to do with me either.

"Would you like some air M? Maybe you'd like to get a drink?" asks the librarian.

I shake my head and look at my screen.

320 pages, that's 1600 pictures of Lynx.

New document – "Top of the World." Lynx on the mountain, 8 per page, 36 pages = 288. This would have been in Year 7, when I first noticed Lynx.

"Were you able to open any files?" The librarian walks towards me.

Minimise Lynx files.

Open – Avalanches.

She peers at my screen. "Oh fantastic! I've a whole section on avalanches." And she picks lots of large books from the shelves, opens them and places loads of pictures of avalanches in front of me.

Snow and ice and rocks crashing down from high mountains. Blasting! Exploding! Imploding!

Avalanches occur when a rapid flow of snow forces down a sloping surface. Avalanches are typically triggered in a starting zone. The forces on the snow exceed its strength and avalanche. They accelerate rapidly and grow in mass and volume as they entrain more snow and matter.

The Year 9 breaks into a sob again. The librarian walks towards her. "Excuse me M."

I switch back to the Lynx files. Neat, ordered, tidy on the pages and again, again. Someone I love, and I do love him! Which is why this all hurts so much. Such messy, messy feelings, that explode with force around my little body!

The library door opens. Toby enters.

Minimise Lynx files.

He draaaaaaaaaaaaaaggs the chair out from the other side of the desk and sits on the edge of the seat.

"Mum told me to come and see you." I'm shocked. He doesn't normally talk to me at school. "She said to make sure you are OK." This makes me feel like I was on some infectious TB ward, like in one of those old-fashioned hospitals which we learnt about in PSE. "I hate it in here M. How can this be better than going to lessons?"

I would rather be in lessons than sat here in the infectious ward.

"What are these?" He looks at the avalanche books and I look to the floor. He flicks through some of the pages and says, "Cool." I focus on my shiny, black, ballet pumps. The avalanches make me edgy.

"How long you in here for?" he asks, like this is a prison visit.

I shrug my shoulders.

"*Why* are you even in here M? This is ridiculous."

I know that. He flicks through *Avalanches – Nature's Way.*

"I don't like Shaznia and Nev or Lara. Why would you even hang out with them? What's wrong with Joe? He's really cool. You should just hang out with him." And I do like Joe but he's not a girl, and a girl needs girlfriends to talk about girl things like boys and love…well…that's what I'd hoped…

I want to say sorry to Toby. Sorry for all the trouble I have caused him, and how my anxiety means he's never in and he always seems so angry and I didn't mean for Dad to leave, and I try to get the word out.

But then he says it,

"Sorry Sis."

I look at him.

"I know you are on your own a lot, at home."

I nod.

"We could do something at the weekend. Take Bella out?"

I nod.

"You know that Year 10 boy…"

I look at my shoes. I am cringing. Stop! I don't want to talk about this with Toby!

"Joe's much cooler."

CRinging.

"Just saying...I've got a hockey match. They're waiting in the mini bus... So I better go. See you later...tonight or maybe tomorrow... It's a late one 'cause it's over in...Canterbury..." And he goes to tap my shoulder and I don't like to be touched, so I pull away.

"See you later, Sis," and Toby leaves.

I open the laptop and get back to copying and pasting the pictures of Lynx. My new file is called "Celebrations at the Club House." Lynx looks tired and he's got a streak of mud on his face and is wearing a blue puffer jacket, and he is smiling, right at the camera. I think this is maybe my favourite picture of him, of all time. I copy 8 on each page and create 568 pages for this file.

The bell screeches through my body and interrupts my work and the librarian walks towards me.

Minimise Lynx files.

"Looks like she got delayed M. I'll chase her up, OK? So come here tomorrow morning and I'll talk to Mr Bray and see about getting you some work. This isn't right, is it?"

I shrug my shoulders. The truth is I just want to get home and see if I can find any more photos of Lynx. He represented the school in athletics last year, maybe there are pictures of him mid-air, jumping over hurdles!

★ ★ ★

Joe catches up with me as I walk home.

"Did you get my text last night?"

I nod.

"Oh…you didn't reply?" he asks/states. He asked how much longer I was going to be in the library and I didn't know the answer, so I didn't reply.

"So, when are you getting out of Holloway Prison?"

?

"It's like a prison for women, in London somewhere… Joke."

I throw him an angry look.

"Bad joke," he adds, "but you know what, M, it's like a violation of your human rights being stuck in there all day." And I wait for him to say "Joke" again or "Funny misunderstanding." And I'm glad he doesn't because he's right. That is how it's beginning to feel.

"What are you *doing* in there all day?"

He wouldn't understand.

"I'll bring you some of the History handouts. We did all this stuff on Pompeii, which is this whole town that lived under a volcano and when the volcano blew and exploded all these people couldn't run or hide and they got covered in ash and preserved and they were doing ordinary things like cooking or taking the dog out and you can still see all their bodies in the moment of death and they are frozen or baked, cooked in time, and Miss Wilson says we might go there for our Year 11 trip."

And he keeps talking about the exploding volcano and I try to block it out and see M in The Mirror Shop. M in the superMarket.

And we arrive at my house.

"I could come in and copy out some of the work for you?"

"I need to go in." And I walk up towards my front door.

"I could take Bella round the block."

"M…" He calls out and I turn.

"Nothing… I'll go to the park or the library…"

I need to get back to the Lynx files.

★ ★ ★

KNOCK KNOCK KNOCK KNOCK KNOCK KNOCK

"What are you doing M?" Mum asks as she enters my little room, uninvited. "Can't you at least answer me?"

Minimise Lynx files.

Bella barges in too, wagging her tail.

"What are you doing? Are you watching Skylar?"

I don't reply. I don't want to lie, but I don't want her to know what I am really doing. This is for me. This is private. Am I not entitled to *some* privacy?

"Will you take Bella out? Why do you watch so much Skylar? Have you seen Toby? Has he texted you or rung you?"

Which questions am I supposed to answer?! Bella flops beside me and presses her big, reassuring Labrador weight against my legs.

"Has Toby rung you? Texted you?"

Toby never texts or rings me. I shake my head and I just want her to go, so I can get on with looking at Lynx on the French Trip, but she says if I don't go down for dinner she'll take my laptop away.

I quickly eat the fish fingers. Bella follows my fork with her eyes.

Plate to my mouth.

Plate to my mouth.

Plate to my mouth.

Mum keeps talking about another counsellor, called Fern, but I don't want another counsellor.

"Did you see Miss Twinnings today?" I shake my head. Mum **SLAMS** the plates in the sink. I slip back to my room and she shouts up the stairs that Bella needs to go out, but I have to get back to the pictures.

And I am creating a new world. A kind of MOLW. And this is an activity that keeps me busy and close to the person I love. And maybe in some funny kind of way I might bring him back to me… In fact that is what is happening. I am keeping him close, and maybe this is some kind of relationship? If I hadn't been so stupid, I might have him here, beside me. Sitting on the edge of my bed. Kissing each other. Or maybe we'd be holding hands on the way home from school.

KNOCK KNOCK KNOCK KNOCK KNOCK KNOCK

I am copying pictures from the Welsh Mountain Adventure Week. Lynx trying to balance on some rocks and it's titled "The Scary Descent." How brave.

I don't think I could ever climb a mountain. My brave Lynx.

"M!" She opens the door.

Minimise Lynx files.

"I've been calling you for 10 minutes. Seriously, M, are you deaf? Do you know anything about Toby?"

"No," I say quietly.

"Right, so there is a voice in there somewhere?"

Bella bursts in. She's got lots of energy. She needs a walk.

"Are you still watching Skylar? Have you seen Toby this evening?" I shake my head and cuddle Bella.

"I don't remember him saying he was going out and he's not answering his phone. Has he texted you?"

I shake my head.

"Has he rung you?"

I shake my head.

"It's late." I look at the clock: 9.00. "He should be home or have at least rung." She and Bella exit and I hear Mum on the phone. She is talking to Dad.

"I haven't lost our son! I'm just trying to find out where he is… For God's sake, Simon, it's not *that* late."

I return to Lynx smiling. 458 files × 20 per page = 9160 smiles. And that is one of the most beautiful things I can think of. 9160 smiles. I smile.

I can hear Dad's voice downstairs. I look at my clock: 10.30. Dad must have come over from The Oval.

KNOCK KNOCK KNOCK KNOCK KNOCK KNOCK KNOCK KNOCK KNOCK KNOCK

I shut my laptop.

"M. Can I come in?" asks Dad. Then LOUDER, "M, please. Can I come in?"

And then Mum's voice,

"M, darling. We need to talk to you." The door opens slowly and she says to Dad, "She's not really talking at the moment."

And he says, "Jesus, Amanda, Toby's missing and M's not talking. What the hell is going on here?" Then he turns his attention to me and says, "Just checking in with you. When did you last see Toby?" I don't want to answer and get it wrong and make this whole situation worse, as usual. "Please M, you won't get into any trouble."

This is good to hear.

"Honestly, honey," says Mum, "we won't tell you off." Mum picks up my clock and says, "Point to when you last saw Toby." I point to 12.00.

"And did he say he was doing anything tonight?"

I nod, and Mum's voice gets all high and quick and says,

"Where M? And what, what did he say he was doing?!"

Where or what? And I can't talk. I can't do it. They can't make me talk because everything will go wrong. Anxiety, now in my little pink room, shaking me, making my head hurt, and it's scratching at my skin and I'm tensing up and I tap my face.

They are in *my* room and I want them to go now. And I feel trapped in *my* own little room and it's Wednesday night. Dad is in The Oval on Wednesday nights and this is *my* safe space and they are in it and I hear Dad say,

"Type it," and he opens my laptop and I **SLAM** the lid down.

"Careful M!" says Mum, and Dad grabs some of my pink heart note paper and knocks my notebooks and pencils around my desk and says,

"Please M, write down where he is." And I need them out and Anxiety is right in my face, and I know it wants to shove me about and rattle me and derail me.

And I take a deep breath in.

Tonight is not as it should be! I rearrange the pencils and notebooks.

"M, please, can you stop doing that!" says Mum.

And I want to shout but I'm caving in now. Anxiety is pummelling at me and my insides are turning in on themselves and my shaking is getting worse.

"This is important M! We need to know where our son is!" continues Mum, and I think, shouldn't *they* know? Why are they stressing me out with all these questions?? I haven't lost Toby. They've crashed into my space and are throwing questions and confusion around! It's bouncing off the walls and the ceilings and hitting at me! Hard!

"M. I'm really disappointed that you can't just write down or speak." If they just give me some space I could sit at my desk and write it down. Can't they just get out?

Mum is crying.

I don't want Mum to be upset. I don't want her to cry. She walks into the landing saying,

"Can't she just co-operate?"

And Dad goes after her and Anxiety leaves the room too.

"I can't believe you haven't kept tabs on where our son is?"

"Oh! This is my fault is it?" replies Mum.

"I would have thought it is your responsibility, so yes."

Then I can take some deep breaths and write.

Hockey Canterbury

And take the note out to the landing. Mum reads it and says,

"I just wish, **wish**, you could have done that earlier M. James's mum should know where they are" and she walks downstairs making a call, and Dad says,

"If you'd have just said or written that two hours ago I wouldn't have had to drive from The Oval and there would have been a lot less fuss and stress."

Fuss, fuss, fuss and I've been told off. I did as they asked but still they told me off.

Broken promise.

* * *

I sit at the top of the stairs and listen to Mum and Dad.

"Yes, he's at a hockey tournament. James's mum said she's arranged to drop him off…it's a late one, apparently…"

"Didn't you know?"

"Yes, well, now I remember, there's a letter sent home…it's in the drawer."

MUM AND DAD SILENCE

"I think it needs to be a bit more organised here, Mandy."

"Oh right, because you're so organised? I couldn't get in this room with your bloody guitars with no strings and albums strewn all over the floor. Do you really think you've a right to talk to me about organisation?"

"Always attacking, Amanda."

MUM AND DAD SILENCE

"When did he start playing hockey?" asks Dad.

"He doesn't. He's volunteering to help with the team, on away matches. He doesn't like being here very much."

"It's a bit of a mess Mandy."

"Right, and you've got nothing to do with that?"

"At least when I lived here we knew where our kids were."

"Oh Simon, can we just NOT argue again please. It's just a bad evening. A very bad evening… Do you want a glass of wine?"

"I better not, I'm driving… Unless I stay?"

"I'll make you a cup of tea." And I hear Mum put the kettle on and **SLAM** cupboard doors and Dad asks,

"Do you think it would help…if…you know, I was here more?"

"What?"

"Sort a few things out in the house. Sort that cupboard door, that you're always having to slam shut, and have you fixed the windscreen wiper on your car yet?"

"Not yet…I'm pretty busy, you know."

"I was thinking maybe I could spend more time here."

AND guitars and clutter and arguments zoom into my thoughts at 100 miles per hour! Broken guitar strings ping and shiny slippy album covers slide about in my head! Their voices go really quiet, so I have to go down a few more steps to hear them speak.

"Simon, are you serious?"

"Yes."

"You never lifted a finger when you were here. And now you want to mend a cupboard door?"

"I knocked up a few meals."

"About twice a year."

"OK…so maybe I could have done more."

"A *lot* more."

"We were together a long time. I mean we have got two kids and maybe they deserve us to try a bit more and keep the family together."

Then Mum's voice gets really loud. I go back up a few steps.

"God! Were you so oblivious to how much I tried to keep this family together?"

"Yes, but M did put a strain on us at times."

STRAIN STRAIN STRAIN

And Dad continues,

"And I've had lots of time to think and I know it's not *all* her fault but…"

ALL? And I can *feel* the force of Mum's voice interrupting Dad. She's like a tsunami and Dad does not stand a chance in the wake of her words.

"I took M to the hospital. I fought with doctors. I fought with psychologists when you didn't believe there was anything wrong."

WRONG WRONG WRONG

"And, Simon, *I* fought to get her diagnosed, I fought to change her primary school when she was being bullied. ME. I did it."

FOUGHT FOUGHT FOUGHT

"AND Simon, what did you do? WHAT did you do? You sold a few second-hand records on a website, rolled a few cigarettes and sat on that bloody sofa for about 20 years, waiting for a record company to sign you up, for a non-existent five million pound record deal."

MUM AND DAD SILENCE

Then Mum comes in with a second wave.

"Life on your *mum's* sofa getting tough, Simon? Is that what this is all about?"

"No. Life at Mum's is pretty comfy…and a lot less hassle. This is about me missing you all. OK? Is that clear, Amanda? I am missing my family, and before you attack me again, just remember, you were not perfect and you dominated this family worrying and talking about *our* daughter. It was non-stop. I mean, why do you think Toby is out all the time? You didn't have a complete monopoly on worrying about her, you know."

"But you didn't believe me! That something was the matter."

"No, of course! I didn't want to! But I can see now that she…"

"Has autism," says Mum.

"Yes."

The fault lines between them seem to have just got deeper.

MUM AND DAD SILENCE

Dad breaks the silence with quiet words.

"I'll call tomorrow. I was just offering to help out a bit more. I didn't mean for us to have a big row."

"Right…" replies Mum.

I hear Dad pick up his car keys, so I disappear back up the stairs to my little pink room. And I thought it might be good for them to fix the breaks, but I don't know if they can. If he came back would he tell me off and bring back all his guitars and records and get angry and live on the sofa again?

I go back to my room and copy and paste. Copy and paste. Copy and paste.

Part 2

Wobbly World

Autism is the hardest boss.

★ Chapter 15 ★

Like a painting or story it acknowledges the way I feel. Makes it real – not all curled up inside my head and my stomach and my heart, I am part of it. In the process. I'm practically at the New Year's Eve party! I'm almost sitting next to him in the club house and being part of his life. I go through my files and the systems of images I have created.

My library but the best subject ever. My library. My world. And I don't want to share it. I just love him and seeing him a thousand times, 10,000 times! And more is a good thing, and this is something I am good at and am getting right. I'm getting *something* right and it is something beautiful. I don't think anyone would understand. No one seems to understand that I don't like being touched or that I don't get their jokes or that I don't like noises. People don't seem to believe me. Like I'm constantly lying. And I'm tired of feeling like I have to defend myself or feel attacked and doubted all the time.

I hear the CRASH of Miss Twinnings' entrance through the library door and a document is presented to me.

"So the procedure is that you read the document and sign."

As a result of the above-mentioned student's behaviour on Monday January 24th, which involved breaking St. Andrew's Code of Conduct Policy: Section 2:

- Challenging and redirecting inappropriate actions, behaviour, attitudes and language.

- Failed to move around the school in an orderly way.

- Did not remain on the school campus during school hours and/or keep to permitted areas.

As of Monday January 31st the above-mentioned student will report to Miss Twinnings before and after school to plan and assess the school day and ensure that the student is working within St. Andrew's Code of Conduct.

Signature _____
Member of staff

Signature _____
Named student

And I read it, but it doesn't make sense to me, and I can hear Miss Twinnings talking about me to the librarian, like I'm not in the room.

"She's on the autistic spectrum, so struggles with nuances, so hopefully these direct instructions will help, *this time*."

Nuances

And she keeps talking about her Autism Awareness training.

Nuances

I get up and look at the dictionary.

Nuance

[noun, plural nuances]

A subtle difference or variation in colour or tone. A very slight difference in expression, meaning, response.

And I think that I *do* notice all the different colours and tones. I notice more than anyone else!

"Have you signed it yet?" calls Miss Twinnings.

I return to the desk.

"Just sign, there." And Miss Twinnings indicates to the dotted line.

But this doesn't make sense to me.

"May I suggest you sign, as you are in quite a bit of trouble already and I think it's best we get you back into lessons and learning ASAP."

I sign.

"OK, so back to your timetable after lunch, OK?"

Is this what I have been waiting for? This *agreement*? I've signed my name but I don't agree. What choice did I have?

I don't want to leave the library, but of course I *do* want to leave the library. I can't stay here for ever, because I want to be normal and go to lessons and learn.

Stress PUMPS PUMPS PUMPS through my veins. I can feel the chemical reactions in my body. Tiny cells being flooded with sharp, hissing, stress.

Code of Conduct. What's wrong with my conduct? What is moving about the school in an orderly way? Am I not orderly? And this doesn't mention how I am going to get to the maths corridor, and this will all happen again because I still can't get to lessons. Nothing has changed and I hate change, but there is no change for the good here? It's just me having to try and FIT IN again! And I can't! I can't fit in!

"Ruby Clarke in Year 9 is having an allergic reaction so I need to rush." And she crashes out the library doors. The librarian sits opposite me.

"M, you know you can come here any time you want. You are always welcome in the library." If I go back to the lessons I will see Shaznia, and she was there on Saturday and witnessed what I did.

And I take some deep breaths.

And she wronged me. Badly. "Shaznia was right, you are weird!"

"And I know you don't like talking...at the moment, but you can talk to me when you feel ready M."

My throat constricts. My mouth is dry. Really dry. I can't get enough oxygen to my lungs, my limbs, my vital organs. I am light headed. If I can't breathe I can't live. Will Anxiety kill me?

An avalanche is slipping and S
l
i
d
i
n
g

and **RUMBLING** inside me. I tap my cheeks.

"M, are you OK?"

A meltdown is happening...

"Count to ten M. In your head."

"Shaznia was right, you are weird!"

An implosion inside of me creeps. She hands me a plastic cup of cold water.

"Take 10 sips M, count them."

1, 2, 3, 4, 5, 6, 7, 8, 9, 10

And I close my eyes and breathe with control and feel the air travel through me, and I try to slow the force, the fear inside that is trying to accelerate and widen and take me over.

"Ten more sips M."

1, 2, 3, 4, 5, 6, 7, 8, 9, 10

And slowly, slowly I still the force that wants to control me.

Deep breath in.

It could all crash back at any moment but, temporarily, there is a stillness.

"Stay here for the rest of the day M."

I open my eyes.

"When I get anxious, I freeze." I look into her eyes, briefly. "It's horrible, I know… Look, I don't know much about what has happened over the past few days or weeks for you M, but step by step, little by little, things will get better. It's been lovely having you here in the library. You seem like a lovely young woman to me and I don't think everyone understands what you are going through. You must feel like you're very alone."

I nod, slightly. I don't want to disrupt my body and risk setting off the avalanche again.

"You can come to the library any time you want. You're always welcome here. What's your first lesson tomorrow?"

And I write ART.

"Do you like Art?"

I nod.

"Start the plan tomorrow. Tomorrow could be the start of a new and good period of your life M."

Tomorrow…

I like the librarian a lot but I don't believe her.

I am the prey in a world of predators.

★ Chapter 16 ★

Registration was bearable. Joe gave me another Twix and it was good to know the safety of the library was there. A haven. A bolt hole. A sanctuary. Anxiety had chased me the whole way to school, but I stayed focused on the squares of time I had to get through and it kept a distance from me. The constant presence of Shaznia, Lara and Nev sitting, hanging behind me was dark and nasty, unpleasant, but I was wearing NO FACE securely and finding some ability to go on. NO FACE, detaching me further from this difficult world.

Mr Bray called me aside as we filed out to Art.

"You OK M?"

I look towards the door. This is making me late.

"Try your best today, mate. I know Miss Twinnings has spent a lot of time with you this week and put a plan together to help you."

Really?

"Sometimes it is just about facing into things." And then he talks about *turning things around and putting my best foot forward*. And I'm going to be late for Art. Art starts at 9.15am. If I go now I'll make it on time. Mr Bray is still talking about how he's had his own personal setbacks, when he was a teenager, but they actually ended up being a *blessing in disguise*. And he's talking in fridge magnet language and I hate it! When will he release me?

"I never thought I'd get back on track again after my parents' divorce but –"

I exit. I have to go. Art starts at 9.15am. And I hear Mr Bray calling after me,

"M, I was in the middle of my sentence…"

I arrive, out of breath, at 9.15am as Miss King is turning off the lights and everyone is settling into their seats.

"Hurry up M," says Miss King as I work my way carefully, in the dim light, over bags and coats strewn on the floor. "I'm projecting some of the world's finest paintings on the white board this morning, so prepare to be amazed 8B." I keep working my way towards the empty seat beside Joe, at the front of the class.

"M's late!" shouts out Nev. "I didn't think you liked being late."

Giggles fill the classroom.

I'm not late.

"Careful M! Ouch!" shouts Nev. "Miss King, M's bag hit my arm. It's like she's got bricks in it or something."

"Be careful M," says Miss King.

I *am* being careful. My bag hardly touched her.

"Miss! M has broken Nev's arm," shouts out Lara. "It looks really serious Miss. She needs to go to hospital. NOW! It's an emergency."

Giggles emit from the darkness.

"I'm sure the emergency can wait till *after* Art," says Miss King.

Finally I reach the safety of my seat and I am worried that I might fall asleep in the darkness. I hadn't slept the night before. My eyes were heavy but then that all changed. My eyes went from heavy to wide and awake and alive!

"So this one is Sunflowers by Vincent Van Gogh," announces Miss King.

And I was struck. Just like being love struck.

I had no idea something so utterly beautiful could exist and I could feel myself slipping…disappearing, sinking into these orange colours and fragile textures. To celebrate these flowers and to hold them in such high regard! How? How can a human paint like this? And Miss King was explaining about the shapes and movement of brush strokes and then she announced, "Starry Night." And a new painting by the same artist appears before me. I gasp! Little electric explosions fire off all round my body. It's like nothing I'd ever seen before and my eyes were sharpened! I felt awake. Wide awake. Excited. Waves of sadness and joy sweep over me. How come such beauty makes me want to cry? And I am willingly being taken over by this because he has painted what I feel when I look at the night sky in my little back garden in Sevenoaks.

I can feel tears building behind my eyes. A tear that is made of water that might have come from the stream in this beautiful painting that might have rolled down the mountain in the town and then evaporated into the sky and travelled over time and distance andbecome part of me! A whole new exquisite world before me! So much sky! So vast! And the town under the night sky was little because it's the sky that is important, and I wondered if Van Gogh was like me and could feel and sense the vast sky. He must! Maybe there is a place for me? If other people like this exist in the world? Like the person who put the benches out in Sun Cottage. Maybe. Maybe I could find a place in this world, and I want to get closer to this picture, be nearer, and I sit forward, like needing to turn the volume up on a song that you love. I want more of it.

And I felt a soft thud on the side of my head.

This is the most wonderful thing I have ever seen… That isn't a tree or a *real* starry sky! And my little existence is transported somewhere else! Somewhere new! This picture *is* nature, and I wasn't expecting that when I left the house this morning, being chased by Anxiety.

Giggles seep out from the darkness.

And I notice my cellophane-wrapped cheese sandwich on the table in front of me.

And I don't want to take myself away from the 11 stars and the glowing moon and I hear Joe's voice cut through the moonlit little village.

"NOOO!" And I turn to see what's happening in the art room but it's dark, so I go back to the night sky! And I can hear Joe saying,

"Give it back."

Maybe this painting is heaven! When people talk about heaven they point to the sky. Maybe this is what they mean! But then heaven is here on this earth! And it's about finding heavenly moments while you're on this earth rather than waiting till you're dead. It's here all the time in the sky and we're all part of it! I'm part of it! Connected up!! And I know that!!! I know that!!!!

And I hear Shaznia and Nev and Lara and I think I'm really not in heaven any more.

"Oh my God M!"

"Christ, this is mental."

"Shaznia was right, you are weird!"

Miss King is telling everyone, "Be quiet, and Joe sit down! Do you hear me Joe? Sit down." Miss King turns the light on and I can see they have my laptop and everyone is scrambling around the screen trying to look.

"Stop being such a cow Shaznia," yells Joe.

"Joe, enough!" shouts Miss King, but Joe isn't listening.

"You just can't leave her alone, can you? You really are a complete cow." But Shaznia isn't listening to Joe or Miss King. She just keeps scrolling through all the files on my laptop.

"It's mental," says Shaznia, and Joe goes over and looks, and I know what they are looking at, and Miss King is looking at the screen now and Shaznia keeps clicking through files and saying,

"Oh my God! There are like thousands and thousands."

"And like why is this all 'Lynx'? Do you call Matthew Phillips 'Lynx'?" asks Nev.

"It's her love name for him," says Lara, laughing and watching more and more files and pictures open on to the screen.

Joe's face changes and he steps back.

"Give it back to her." Joe's voice is quieter. "You really are cruel."

"Did you take this laptop from M's bag?" asks Miss King.

SILENCE

"Well Shaznia?"

"Yeah, but it's a school laptop, so officially it doesn't belong to M, it belongs to all of us."

"Right, get outside Shaznia and we'll talk at the end of the lesson."

"Turns out it was an act of public safety." And Nev starts giggling.

"Someone better let Matthew Phillips know he's got a stalker," adds Shaznia. "I mean *Lynx*."

Laughter rises from everyone.

"ENOUGH. You have totally disrupted my lesson – now get outside."

"I think you'll find it's M and her stalking activities that have disrupted the lesson, not me."

"OUT! Now." Her chair scrrraaaaaapes on the floor. She drags herself out the art room.

"I don't see why *I* should be leaving." And she **SLAMS** the door.

"Joe, sit down!" Miss King shouts. "And DO NOT, I repeat DO NOT, shout out in my class again. Is that clear Joe?"

He sits down beside me.

"Answer the question Joe. Is that clear?"

He nods.

"Right, clearly, this class cannot be trusted to work with the lights out. I thought there was a higher level of maturity in 8B but I was mistaken. So, books out and write me a list of the techniques Van Gogh uses. I've given you at least ten. So let's see who was listening."

And there is a silence in the room. And I can't really see the picture of Starry Night very well because the flickering fluorescent lights are throwing out their harsh nauseating glow, but I wish I was there, in that little village, far, far away from St. Andrew's Academy.

And of course The Beast of Anxiety is circling me, bearing its sharp teeth, reminding me that an attack is always imminent... But I secure NO FACE. To help me operate. To stop me from imploding and curling up in a little ball on the art room floor.

Joe is writing the list. His face is bright red and he looks ruffled. His breathing is shaky. Is he feeling anxious? Or upset? He seems distant. I never meant to upset Joe. Have I upset Joe?

The classroom is very quiet. I watch as Miss King goes through files on the laptop. And I see her mouth the word,

"GOD."

She looks at me and snaps,

"M. Are you writing the list?"

I'm not.

"I sincerely hope you were listening to the ten techniques I mentioned earlier." But I wasn't listening because I was looking at the most beautiful pictures I have ever seen.

And I'm scared. Not of Nev or Lara or Shaznia, or of what's "going to happen" next, because I am sure something is "going to happen."

But I'm scared of myself.

Tomorrow was meant to be a good day. I knew it was unlikely.

I could suggest that you walk in my shoes for a day but that's not enough. Try putting my brain in your head, that's the only way you'll ever understand autism.

★ Chapter 17 ★

I'm focused on the crack of light coming from under Mr Crane's office door. Shadows break the slant of light. What's he doing? Signing important documents? Phoning important people? Is he in there preparing to change my life? Why do we have to wait? I was told this was urgent, and now Debbie, the Head's PA, said Mum and me need to wait five minutes. I dread the five minute phrase. When I'm left to hang in eternity. It should go on the Useless Clock.

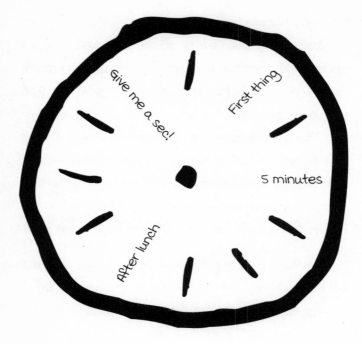

I go through the list of Head Boys' and Girls' names on the large wooden plaque by Mr Crane's door.

1962 PETER HOLMES

1963 PHILIP SANDERSON

1964 OLIVER FITZPATRICK

If I go in that office I'm really not sure I will survive. I look at my shaking hands.

1965 CRISPIN TAYLOR

Mr Crane's meanness is seeping out from under the door and into the funny foyer area. Why are Mum and I waiting? He said this was a matter of "the highest importance." So what is he doing in the office that is more important than this? Has someone else done something worse than me? I thought I'd done the worst thing ever in the history of this school. What is of higher importance?

Carpet tiles.

Coins.

Ceiling squares. Again, again.

1966 DAVID LATHAM

1967 GERRARD O'DONNELL

Anxiety is ripping at my throat and I judder as I breathe out.

1968 GUY COOK

1969 TERRENCE DAVIES

I'm struggling to breathe in and I go back to the list of names.

1970 CLAIRE LYLES. A girl! A girl!

1971 SEAN O'NEIL

Debbie, the school PA, asks if I am OK, but she's keeping a distance from me. Does she think I'm contaminated or she'll catch what I have? Can you catch what I have? Am I infected? Did I catch it? I know websites and leaflets say I'm born with "it" and it can't be cured, but are they sure? In History we learnt about people dying of diseases that you can cure now with penicillin and other wonder drugs, so maybe this is a disease and it will be cured one day. I've spent a lot of time at doctors and hospitals, so maybe I am ill and contagious? Who did I catch this off? I pull my fingers. My knuckles reassuringly crack... Mum replaces my hands onto my knees.

My face is red and I tap my cheeks.

I pull my knuckles again. No crack. I pull harder.

"Stop it," says Mum in a tight whisper.

I clasp my hands together on my lap.

1972 LEWIS BAILEY

"Take a deep breath M," she whispers.

"Would you like some water?" Debbie asks me.

I shake my head.

"Yes, Debbie, if you don't mind, please give her some," says Mum.

I don't want water!

"Sip it, slowly," says Mum. I do, but it's freezing, and icy pain zig-zags through my brain.

"Think about what you can say to Mr Crane M. You've got some serious explaining to do and I am *fed up* with this silence nonsense. OK? You need to explain what the hell you've been playing at. Not talking is going to make things a lot worse M."

I'm not convinced.

"And you owe *me* an explanation. I trusted you on that laptop and I've given so much freedom and look what you do. And you never did tell me what happened that Saturday. When you disappeared on your own. Have you got some strange double life going on M?"

Maybe I do have a **strange double life.**

"AND…" says Mum really loudly. Debbie looks up. Mum whispers again, tightly. "…I've had to leave work early for the second time this week M." I don't want Mum to lose her job. She is so very upset. So I think about how I can explain…

I didn't realise I was doing wrong. The pictures were not meant to hurt Lynx and I certainly didn't want him to know and now I imagine someone has told him, and if he's upset he shouldn't be. Making the files and the folders made me feel better, but now I feel worse, and I am not weird and I am truly sorry for causing trouble. It has never been my intention to cause trouble. I just want to learn and have friends, but I'm struggling here! And I'm figuring from all the leaflets and websites I've read, Mr Crane, you probably don't get anxiety like me, and The Beast of Anxiety doesn't pace after you and chase you and rip at you and scream in your ear or claw your nerves and beat you to submission, because if it did, I think you'd realise I live my life differently to you and this all makes sense to me.

That's what I'll say.

I pull at my knuckles.

Please, please, bell, don't ring! I don't want everyone to pass by and look at me like some kind of exhibit. I tap my face. Inside I am screaming. Anxiety is squeezing my internal organs and my heart is beating so fast. I wonder if I might have a heart attack.

Mum replaces my hands to my lap.

Tears are building, but I don't want to cry now. I tap my face and catch sight of my reflection in the trophy cabinet. I look scared. *I* can see that. Can anyone else see my fear? I thought you should be kind to people or animals that are scared and I'm scared of so much! But most of all, I am scared of Anxiety. I talked about this with Fiona. Fiona. Fiona. Big empty loneliness sits in my tummy. Hollow, black and eternal. A tear escapes from my eye.

"Crying won't help now M," says Mum. Her lips are tighter.

Help. What would help at this point? MOLW. The pull is strong. The lure is tempting. Fiona and I had talked about MOLW and how I should try and stay in *this* world and work problems out, systematically, methodically, with order and negotiation…but walking through the quiet street of the small town under the starry night is where I crave to be – then the door opens and the foyer area is flooded with light and Mr Crane stands in the doorway, circled in white, bright light. I can't see his face, just a dark silhouette. He doesn't say anything, just disappears back into his room. Mum stands and follows him into his office. She looks back at me and in a sharp voice says, "Come on." Debbie keeps looking at her screen but then I see her eyes dart up and she looks at me as I exit the foyer to the office… Anxiety accompanies me.

The office smells of polish and old wood and I immediately focus into the gold embossed books with dates and letters. A–B, C–F, G–K, L–M, N–P, Q–T, U–Z neatly shelved in the wooden book case. M stuck in the middle. A very beautiful, gold M, embossed onto a navy leather book spine, but still stuck in the middle. Elegant M. It would take a lot of work for M to get to the beginning or the end of the alphabet. It's impossible. M's been put in the middle. Trapped. But who put M in the middle? Who made that decision? Everyone accepts that M is in the middle and that's just the way it is. It doesn't have to be. It's not like numbers; they have to be in that order. People would die if numbers changed their order, but not letters. The world wouldn't stop if M changed its place in the alphabet. But beautiful, symmetrical, squeezed-in M is stuck in a place it's been put.

The window is slightly open and a breeze flows through the room. I breathe in this fresh air. I have been in this room four times in the past two years and I've studied the school motto over Mr Crane's desk:

STRIVE NOT ONLY FOR YOURSELF BUT FOR
YOUR SCHOOL AND FELLOW HUMAN.

This time in Mr Crane's office feels different. Mum *and* Dad have never been called before. Mum but never Dad.

"Will your husband be joining us?" asks Mr Crane.

"No, he can't make it."

"Work?" enquires Mr Crane.

"Well, he's in The Oval and couldn't make it here on time." Mum squirms in the following silence. Then can't resist filling it. "We're separated. He lives there now, but he is still very involved with M and Toby's lives and education."

"I see." And he rearranges a pencil and a note book on his desk. I don't like Mr Crane, but I find his neat row of pens and stack of papers reassuring. "Toby's a high achiever at St. Andrew's."

And I wonder, did Claire Lyles from 1970 ever find herself here? Bet she didn't. She was probably winning the 100 metres and getting A grades in French and Maths. I hate Claire Lyles, but I'm so jealous of Claire Lyles and I want to be Claire Lyles. I bet Anxiety didn't stop her from talking when she accepted her Head Girl Award, and I bet it didn't hunt her down these very classrooms and corridors. She probably bounced confidently down the maths corridor, her pony tail swinging, saying "Hi guys!" to all her friends. I HATE CLAIRE LYLES.

"But I think we have a *few* issues with M," continues Mr Crane, "which need to be addressed today. Including the most recent and concerning event which is unfortunately one in a series of serious matters, which have been brought to my attention over your past two years at St. Andrew's."

"Right," says Mum, straightening herself up in her chair. "I…I…I agree I think we probably do need to talk about some things that have been happening and sort them out. I…I agree Mr Crane, and I'm sure M does too, don't you?"

"Academically, I can see there has been a decline in some of your grades. Which is a shame because you were showing potential towards the end of Year 7. However, I sit here today with a…what I can only describe as a 'pile' of report slips and notes from various staff members on my team. A very concerning pile of papers which does not reflect the type of student I wish to have at St. Andrew's."

Silence. He looks at me. And looks at Mum.

I feel my throat constrict.

"So," he continues, "a selection from the pile." And he reads,

Refusal to enter English room – peeling paint?

Repeatedly refuses to use the maths corridor.

He counts out slips of paper, 1, 2, 3, 4, 5, from December.

Repeatedly late for Maths.

I *can't* use some of the corridors, so I have to go round the long route. I don't want to go to History via the cloakroom! I don't want to be late. I hate being late.

Walking out of a science lesson
halfway through an experiment.

He counts more slips of paper:

4 reports of M walking away when
staff are talking to her.

Refusing to answer to her real name.

And now this – abuse of school laptop
and intimidation of Year 10 student.

HEADMASTER SILENCE

He coughs and then talks like he does in an assembly and about to give the school a speech. OFFICIAL.

"It is one thing when a student at St. Andrew's jeopardises their own education and wellbeing and quite another matter when it directly affects another one of my students."

"Of course," agrees Mum. "The...picture incident is...was...is unfortunate, and I assure you my husband and I are addressing this and –"

"If I may continue and correct you. This is not an incident. If I'm going to be frank with you, and I do believe that is the best way forward here, I need to spell out to you that your daughter's actions have breached the law. The UK law, not school rules."

Anxiety hits my body. A full body blow. Distress courses through my veins, every synapse in my brain is transmitting stress! Sirens screech through me. I am charged with terror. Wired. I want to push that window open and escape through it, but I'm paralysed. I can't raise my hand, let alone climb out a window. And I feel so separate from these two other human beings in this room as I sit, separate in my plastic chair. Is this why Mr Crane doesn't apply the school motto to me? He doesn't strive to understand me? Because I don't feel like his fellow human at all. I'm another species, and I'm outnumbered in St. Andrew's, the world. I'm in *their* territory of laws, rules and codes of conduct.

Mum is stuttering and struggling to get her words out.

"Is it? The law... Can...Mr Crane, should we talk about this without M? You see, she gets very upset, and I'm not sure exactly what you mean. I know the pictures are – wrong, but..."

"I think it's important that she stays and listens to potential consequences. My attitude is if one of my students is capable of a crime, they should take responsibility for their actions."

Prisons. Trapped. Shaznia's aunt says I'm the one with the criminal disease. Sirens screaming.

Judder. MOLW. The pull is strong. The lure is tempting. MOLW... Work problems out, systematically, methodically, with order...but that starry night...

"But what crime? Is there something else?" asks Mum. "Is there something I don't know about?"

"Effectively stalking."

"Stalking?" The word **STALKING** hangs in the air over our heads. Then Mum says,

"Are you calling *my* daughter a stalker?"

"Over 20,000 pictures of the Year 10 boy downloaded onto a school laptop."

"It's a school girl crush. A crush. We've all had crushes."

"20,000."

"All kids are looking at each other on the internet, on their phones, these days. *You* should know that. Bloody hell…we're all probably stalkers!"

"Over 20,000 pictures is not a crush."

I look at the little open gap in the window.

"But it is… It's *her* crush! She likes numbers and patterns and repetition. It's probably how she coped… with liking someone. It's teenage behaviour…and hormones. She doesn't drink in the park like some of the girls in her class or…smoke, and what about some of the pictures kids are looking up these days, have you checked any of their phones??!"

"We are not here to discuss other pupils. I have had to inform Matthew Phillips' parents of this and I have had to stop Mrs Phillips from calling the police."

Mum's head drops and she says,

"No…no."

The moon lights up the paths towards the mountains, the 11 stars shine – bright! And I hear Mum's voice down a French alleyway,

"Hands."

And I replace them onto my lap and I am back in the room. I examine Mr Crane's angular face. His jaw is tense and his nostrils flare when Mum talks. His tiny eyes dart about the room like a bird. He holds his hands tightly in a tense prayer position, which he occasionally releases to straighten the antibacterial hand gel on his desk.

"I spent an hour on the phone convincing Mrs Phillips that this issue could be dealt with *in* the school. The hour I was meant to be leading the Senior Management meeting. Developing plans for the academic success of my students. But instead I was trying to convince a parent *not* to send the police round to my school. I do not want police at my school."

"What was she thinking? Why would she do that?"

"Police issues within a school are not desirable."

"But that's ridiculous! Don't you think she is over-reacting?"

"Police cars outside the school gates doesn't send out a great message."

"No, no, of course I understand, but M hasn't meant to cause any trouble here! Those girls in her class are upsetting her, and the counsellor she sees is leaving. She needs extra support...for her autism."

"Autism?"

"Yes, it's in her folder. We've spoken about it before and the email was sent round."

"Yes, I am aware of the email, but I'm not really interested in your daughter's...autism." And he flaps his hand in the air as he says autism. He's just dismissed autism. He flicked it out of his life. Out the little gap in the window. "It's her behaviour that is of great concern to me."

"But her autism and behaviour are...linked!"

"OK. Let's just park up for a moment."

Park?

"I've been working in education for over 30 years now and I've dealt with many young people with 'issues,' and my experience has led me to the conclusion that home life is always the root of a student's 'issue.'"

"What do you mean?" Mum stiffens her spine.

"I'm never popular for saying this, but I am not in this job to make friends. Sometimes we have to look to events that are happening in the home, in the family, to help us understand our son or daughter's unsocial or inappropriate actions within the school environment. Most children and young people are resilient and cope with typical teenage trials – if there is domestic stability."

"Are you saying problems at home have caused this?"

"By your own admission your daughter sees a counsellor, which suggests to me there are problems."

"But...but...the counsellor, she helps M. It's a good thing!"

"The breakup of a family is very traumatic."

"Yes, yes, there have been some upsetting times for us all, but Simon and I are amicable."

"So sometimes we need to look at our circumstances objectively and assess how this affects our child's behaviour." He is now stabbing his desk with his finger.

The stabs stab at me.

"But my daughter has autism. Do you understand exactly what that means?"

"OK, let me be more candid in my response – after working in the education system for over

30 years there isn't much I don't know about teenage behaviour."

"Her autism has nothing to do with me and Simon's relationship." And Mum is nearly crying now.

"And I would like to add that a girl with autism is a very unlikely and rare phenomenon."

"But she's had the diagnosis. From the hospital. She has a…a…letter."

Phenomenon? I tap my face. Mum replaces my tapping, shaking hands to my lap.

"Let's just say over the years I've been aware of many 'fashions' within the medical world. A few years ago she may well have been called ADHD or been told by a consultant that she had a personality disorder even."

"Look, I admit she needs more support and I could…*we* could make things better, but she does have autism."

"Ultimately I have a school to run and your daughter's behaviour needs to fit the Code of Conduct, and at the moment…" and he leans across his desk and looks Mum straight in the eye and says, "…it doesn't."

And I want Mum to stand up and punch him and shout,

"She is autistic and she is obsessive and she lives with anxiety on a daily basis and she fights to get through each day. She hangs onto life and existence by a thread. She spends the day terrified, terrified! Of noises and smells and textures and tastes that we can't even begin to imagine. Autistic! She is AUTISTIC!"

And I really, really think she wants to do this too. I can feel her rising, and sense her on the edge of telling him! Telling him I CAN'T HELP THIS!!!!!!!!! And he says,

"Would you like your daughter to keep attending St. Andrew's?"

She sits back and quietly says,

"Yes, yes I think so… Whatever is right for M."

"Miss Twinnings has given me a copy of the plan she worked on with M. With reference to today's events I have amended the plan to a 9-point agreement."

He hands us both a copy, which makes me think he was never going to listen to my mum about anything, as he's made lots of decisions before we even came into the room – so I was right, he was busy planning and changing my future with these nine points.

9-Point Action Plan

Positive behaviour and discipline are key foundations for a good education at St. Andrew's. Without an orderly atmosphere effective teaching and learning cannot take place. We expect and insist on the highest standards of behaviour by all members of the school community.

Below are nine points, devised and tailored specifically for the student, which need to be agreed to before the student can return to school after their exclusion period.

It is school policy that students have the opportunity to explain their actions before entering into a St. Andrew's Action Plan.

1. On return to school the student is required to talk to an appropriate member of staff for support, when required, e.g. Head of Pastoral Care.

2. Use school building, corridors and classrooms efficiently and effectively.

3. Arrive at lessons on time.

4. Communicate with staff verbally.

5. Communicate with staff and students in a courteous manner.

6. Respect for school equipment. School equipment and facilities to be used for assigned school work only.

7. On no account will the student leave lessons or school premises without

permission from staff and a written
agreement.

8. A return to official name.

9. A weekly meeting with Head of
   Pastoral Care, to review and monitor
   and review conduct, until all the
   below signatories agree a sufficient
   time has passed.

Student's Signature _____

Parents' Signature _____ &

_____

Form Tutor _____**Phil Bray**_____

Head of Pastoral Care _*Miss Jill Twinnings*_

Head Teacher _*Mr M.J. Crane*___

St. Andrew's Academy

I see letters and words, but Anxiety doesn't allow me
to read to the end of sentences. That's what Anxiety
does; it takes you halfway up a mountain and then
dumps you alone.

Or lets you see half the sentence, then pushes its
claws into your eyes.

Anxiety leaves you stranded. It takes you to the
edge of a cliff and pushes you around near a sheer
drop, your footing slips and you really believe that
you might die.

"You will see from this 9-Point Action Plan that you have a week to reflect on recent events. After discussion with Miss Twinnings and the Year 10's parents, I have decided that the best course of action, in this case, is to exclude you for a week."

EXCLUDE?

"Exclude her? I'm not sure that's fair…what about the other girls, who bully M? … Could we maybe see if Simon, M's father, could get here? I could call him again." She reaches into her bag for her phone. "And we could *all* talk about this?"

"At St. Andrew's we have a very clear Code of Conduct, which the majority of my students follow the majority of the time."

"I know but…"

"Don't you understand? If I let one student away with utter disregard of the Code of Conduct, everyone will think they can get away with it."

"But exclude her?"

"You signed a contract when your daughter joined St. Andrew's to support her in following the rules. The document explained the importance of rules and how breaking them will result in consequences."

Mum nods.

"I have a school governors' meeting in Croydon in an hour. So if you'll excuse me, I need to leave. It is Miss Twinnings' role to support you, and she will be your point of call, if you need to discuss anything in the 9-Point Plan." Mr Crane stands and is now putting papers into his briefcase. He looks up at me while checking through a folder. "I am sorry that it has come to this but you need to use this week as an opportunity to reflect on your actions." And he points to the school motto over his desk, which says, "Strive not only for yourself but for your school and fellow human."

"I just wasn't really expecting this, Mr Crane," says Mum. "I think M didn't really understand her actions."

"And this is a week for her to *try* and understand. As you will see from the 9-Point Plan, it is my obligation to ask the student if you have anything you would like to say. Bearing in mind I need to be in Croydon by 3.15." Mr Crane shuts his briefcase, stands up and says, "So is there anything you would like to say M?" And Mum told me I better think of what I can say. I say it.

"I didn't realise I was doing wrong. The pictures were not meant to hurt Lynx and I certainly didn't want him to know, and now I imagine someone has told him, and if he's upset he shouldn't be. Making the files and the folders made me feel better, but now I feel worse, and I am not weird and I am truly sorry for causing trouble. It has never been my intention to cause troub–"

"OK, OK, thank you…" interrupts Mr Crane, but I haven't finished.

"I just want to learn and have friends but I'm struggling here! And I'm figuring from all the leaflets and websites I've read, Mr Crane, you probably don't get anxiety, like a beast." And I can hear Mr Crane saying,

"Stop, stop!"

But I can't stop. Like outside the cinema, when I was talking to Lynx I couldn't stop.

"And it doesn't pace after you and chase you and rip at you and scream in your ear or claw your nerves and beat you to submission because, if it did, I think you'd realise I live my life differently to you and this all makes sense to me." And I finish and gasp for air and try to draw oxygen into my lungs.

"SSSSTOPP. This is exactly the kind of problem we need to address with you. You do not listen to instructions. You continue to talk over me, when I asked you to stop." And then Mum says,

"It was probably what she prepared…in her head. It's how she talks sometimes."

And then he says it. He says my real name.

"From now on my communication with you will be with your proper name. I've had quite enough of playing along with this M business and I think this is a positive step towards adulthood. This meeting is officially over ladies, so if you'll excuse me I need to get to Croydon. After you." And he gestures towards the door.

We stand up. Mum says, "Thank you." And I glance at the beautiful gold embossed M. We leave, walk past Debbie and the water cooler and she keeps typing. She doesn't look up.

Mum asks me, "How do we get out of this bloody hell hole?" And I take her to the exit. Via the cloak room, past the science block, so we don't have to go down the maths corridor.

I live a life on the edge of a cliff and
I'm looking over at clouds below. Is
there warm, inviting water below or
sharp rocks waiting to impale me?

★ Chapter 18 ★

We got in the car. Anxiety got in too. Its presence strong and overbearing in the small space. Like a vicious beast, with no care for me it starts its frenzied attack.

I open the window...maybe Anxiety might get sucked out... No such luck, it hangs on. Clings on to me, tightly.

"Shut the window M, it's freezing." And then Mum keeps talking and talking, but not about what had just happened in the Head's office. Which is still with me.

Mr Crane's meanness.

The humiliation.

The smell of polish.

The gold M.

ALL still with me.

I can't shed it. Mum is now talking about lasagne.

"That's what we'll have M, lasagne for dinner. You'll eat some lasagne won't you? Try?"

Anxiety has pinned me to the seat.

We pull out of the school gates and I wonder if Mum is going to tell me off about the pictures and punish me, but she just keeps talking about lasagne.

"I'll make a big lasagne and then we can have it for tomorrow, or maybe Jackie will come over and have dinner with us. We'll just get on with things like it's a normal week."

NORMAL

I look out the car window.

M in the Milk chocolate poster.

M in Marella's Nail Bar.

M in Book Makers.

M in the old lady's Morrisons bag.

And I haven't finished school properly. I'm leaving and the clock in the car says 2.32. The day is out of order.

M in registration plates.

M in the shape of branches.

M in the arches of a railway bridge we drive under.

M in the Magic FM poster.

"I'll have to call work and get the week off. I'll have a proper chat with Steve… He's not going to be happy…explain it all. I might get it as sick leave or something, or maybe your dad can come and stay. I can't lose this job M."

M is an upside down W in SLOW painted on the road.

M in car names…Mini, BMW.

"We'll go shopping or go into town and do what normal families do."

NORMAL

And she repeats herself, again and again.

"We'll go shopping or go into town and do what normal families do…yeah, shopping."

Like if she keeps saying it she will make us normal.

And she puts on the radio.

"Oh I love this song M." And she sings along.

Anxiety shoving at me. Pushing at me. Pummelling me as I sit in the car seat and I keep trying to find Ms, but it wants me totally.

"Panic on the streets of London. Panic on the streets of Birmingham! This is one of the first songs me and your dad danced to at uni."

And I can't work out if people are happy or sad or angry at the best of times, but this is really confusing. Mum is saying happy things but she's so tense. She is sitting forward on the car seat now and she won't stop talking...or singing.

"But there's panic on the streets of Carlisle, Dublin, Dundee, Humberside, I wonder to myself... You can do a bit of reading and we'll go to a museum. That's what we'll do!" And she **BANGS** on the steering wheel. "A museum and then we'll go to the gift shop, where you can choose a book, an educational book, and read it! So really M it will be better than school. You could argue it will be more educational. Yes, more educational." And she sings again, *"Hang the DJ."*

2.34. I should be in Maths.

"Panic on the streets of Sevenoaks." And she laughs.

Mum's being really weird. I don't like it, and I can't slip away up to my little pink room or in the garden because I'm **stuck** in the car, and Mum is being different and I don't like different. All I want to do is get to my room but we're stuck in traffic. The car is edging along in the queue.

M in a bearded man's Metallica T-shirt.

M in Moroccan Restaurant.

M in the sign to Maidstone.

"Me and your dad loved this band, The Smiths… I wonder to myself… That was like a different life."

Anxiety's assault continues…choking me.

A splattering of rain hits the windscreen and reverberates in my chest.

The rain BEATS harder onto the windscreen. Another layer of noise in my head.

"A week, we'll just try and have a normal week." And the windscreen wiper on the driver's side sticks in the middle of the windscreen, right in front of Mum's face. Mum keeps pushing the lever, by the steering wheel, up and down saying, "Come on! Work!" and she can't see a thing out her side of the windscreen and she keeps saying to me, "What can you see? Am I too close to the car in front?" And I tap my cheeks. How am I supposed to know? Maybe we are.

Blaring, BLARING radio.

Mum winds her window down and tries to drive looking out the window. The rain gets harder.

"Can't you just answer me M? Can't you bloody answer? You're right beside me! You must be able to hear me! Just try. We could have a crash here. This could be a life or death situation and still you tap your face."

DEATH?

"This is an opportunity for you to step up and help me, help yourself M." And then she calls me by my real name. "Mr Crane is probably right, it's time you took a step towards adulthood." And now she's leaning in towards the windscreen and squinting through all the rain drops landing on the window, trying to look round the wiper in the middle of the windscreen. I want to tell Mum to pull over. The cold air has entered the car and is sweeping around the interior. The rain is getting harder and Anxiety is denying me the ability to breathe. Death.

r

a

i

n

radio

wiper screech

singing

PANIC

talking – talking – talking – talking

And then it happens.

2.36

We crash into the car in front.

A hard JOLT. Immediately followed by a heavy **SLAM** into the back of our car and I'm tensed up. Every muscle. Every bone of being is TENSE! Will there be another smash? Are we going to die? Life or death situation. A strange, eerie silence hangs in the car. Anxiety has complete control of me.

"Panic in the streets of London, panic in the streets of Birmingham."

Mum's holding on to the steering wheel just staring at the rain, which BEATS BEATS BEATS on the windscreen. Will I die? Is this it? Am I going to die by the side of the road? I've always believed my life was more fragile than everyone else's so I'm more easily broken…

★ ★ ★

Rocking. Rocking. Soothing rocks. Turns down the volume of all the noise. Gives me focus. Detaches me. Rocking.

KKKKRCHHHHHHHH

The harsh, electronic interference of a police man's radio adds to the layer of sounds and vibrations that are juddering and living, uninvited, in me right now.

Rocking.

He shouts to my mum who is standing on the grass verge,

"Does she always rock?"

Mum doesn't answer, her head is hanging low, and a woman is shouting at her and jabbing her finger. Jab, jab, jab.

3.01

I am rocking. Rocking. Rocking. Soothing rocks. Turns down the volume of all the noise. Gives me focus. Detaches me. Rocking.

I clench my fingers into tight fists. Again and again. The repetition brings a brief flit of stability amongst the chaos.

The passenger door is open and a police man is kneeling beside me.

"Your mum said you're finding this very difficult." His head tilts as he now talks into the radio attached to his uniform.

"Minor RTA Collision on York Street. Over." And a disturbing electronic voice replies,

KKKKERKKKKKKKK *"Need for assistance? Over?"* KKKKKKEERKKK

"Assessing need for medical assistance. No obvious injuries. Young female very distressed. Over."

KKKKKHHHHCKKKK *"Any back up needed? Over."* KKERRCHHH

"Negative. One car needs to be towed. Owner is organising Recovery Company to collect vehicle. Will clear. Over."

KKKKKRKKKK *"Over."* KRKKKKHHHHH

"You've had a nasty shock, haven't you?" he says to me.

It's still raining. Mum is still being jabbed at by the woman.

"Does your neck or back hurt?" he asks. I look into his deep brown eyes. Are they concerned or angry eyes? I just don't know. Is he going to tell me off? Does he know that I've broken the law? Does he know I am a criminal? His navy blue jumper looks rough and scratchy.

Anxiety is still pinning me against the seat.

"Do you think you could get out the car and have a walk about? It might help me work out if you're hurt." I can't move, but it isn't because my spine is cracked or broken. It's Anxiety's constant force that stops me moving. "Take a deep breath," he instructs, and I try. "You're going to have to get out soon, your mum's car needs to go to a garage. I'll take you both home. So you'll be safe. You could start by taking your seat belt off."

Safe. Safe, safe, safe, but I should be in History. It is 3.05 and I should be in my History lesson. Not by the side of York Street.

"I'm going to give you five minutes M," says the police man, "and I'll come back and we'll try again. Keep breathing deeply. It will help."

Five minutes. 3.10. 3.10. No one ever returns in FIVE minutes.

And as he stands he looks at the windscreen.

"Has there been a problem with the wiper?" he calls over to my mum as he walks round the front of the car and inspects it. The horrible finger-jabbing woman continues to jab and shout as my mum raises her head.

Cars pass. They slow down and I see drivers and passengers looking in at me. I rock.

He opens the driver's door and turns the key in the ignition. One wiper kicks into movement, the other doesn't. It's stuck. Stuck. He turns the engine off and calls over at my mum again,

"Were you having problems with this wiper before you crashed into the back of this woman's vehicle?"

Mum freezes. I recognise this fear. He walks over to Mum and says,

"Knowingly driving with reduced visibility is a criminal offence."

There is a terror in her eyes, I recognise this... because in front of her now is a terrible, terrible future, unfolding at great speed. The car crash would be her fault and she'd go to prison. Maybe I'd go to prison, for aiding and abetting a criminal. Like the two puppy thieves in Skylar, season 8, episode 7, who told lies to Law Enforcement Officers about Skylar's Bichon Frise! She'll lose her job and the family would be even more broken up. The jabbing woman marches over and inspects the wiper and shouts,

"She's been dangerous driving. She could kill someone. Her child even!"

And she jabs at me.

"The jolt of the collision may have caused it. I imagine that's the case, isn't it?" says the police man. Mum nods her head and says, quietly,

"Yes."

But it's not what happened. The jabbing woman **BANGS** her fist on the bonnet of our car and shrieks and rants and the police man asks her to calm down or he'll have to caution her, and she SHOUTS,

"INSANE! This lunatic driver causes criminal damage to my car and *I'm* getting a caution?"

Friday's school day hasn't finished as it should. It's 3.20 and I should be walking past the 12 coins now and I count 1–2–3–4–5–6–7–8–9–10–11–12.

I am a frightened cat being chased
by a vicious dog which keeps
catching me and ripping me apart.

✭ Chapter 19 ✭

The police man dropped us off, and as we got out the car he asked if I needed to go to A&E as he thought I might have shock, but Mum said,

"We'd be there every day if we went whenever she had a meltdown. This is every day."

Bella greeted us when we entered, wagging her tail and woofing.

Anxiety enters too.

Usually Mum makes a big fuss of her, but instead she went straight to the fridge and grabbed a bottle of wine. She unscrewed it and poured herself a big glass.

"Sit down M, come on," she said, drinking the wine quickly. "I'll erm...make that lasagne." But I don't want to sit down. I don't want lasagne. I need to go to my room. She opens and slams lots of cupboards. She is still wearing her coat. "Sit down M. It won't take long." And she puts the radio on. "Oh I love this tune. It's just like a nice Friday night eh?" And she sings along,

"Here in my pocket I've got the story of the blues."

"Sit down M." I sit on a kitchen chair, my head buried into my folded arms in front of me, hiding my face and covering my ears, trying to block out Mum slamming doors and drawers and singing.

"Stoory of the bluuueeesss."

"This is another song we used to dance to M!" **SLAM** "OK. So there's no pasta, I'll make you a cheese sandwich. Yeah?" She opens the fridge; the suction sound squeezes at my skull and the clink of the wine bottle on her glass clinks, clinks, clinks in my head.

"We should talk about the...knock...accident... shouldn't we, really?" I can hear her taking a plate out of the dishwasher and running it under the tap. "I know I got a bit annoyed in the car...and the police being there must have made it seem a bit scary," andshe stops and glugs more wine from her glass and then her phone beeps. A text. "Might be

Jackie." And she rushes over to her handbag on the sofa and reads out loud,

> We believe you have been in a collision, ring 0800 254 356 for SuperautoLawyers.

And then she is silent and the song continues.

"You try to get back home, then you realise you've got nothing left to lose!"

And then she cries.

And through her tears she says, "I'll make you that sandwich. Wait there and I'll make you a nice cheese sandwich," and I look up to see her scrolling through her phone and I can hear Jackie's answer phone message and Mum leaves a message:

"Jackie, it's me. I've had a terrible day Jacks. Terrible and I'm a shit mother. I keep trying Jackie, and I know you told me not to try too hard, but I'm sorry. I'm so sorry to leave this message, on a Friday night and everything, but I'm having some wine and if you get this message tonight call or come over...if you fancy it, but you probably don't fancy being with me tonight and I'll probably end up falling

asleep soon. Oh Jackie, M's headmaster. He's such a bully. I'm rambling, I'll stop now. Or maybe you're at your cottage… So you probably won't get this message… If you are, sorry, love you Jacks. Speak soon…sorry."

The song finishes: *"Story of the bluuuues."*

Mum's crying upset me. Another layer of noise. An upset noise. A distressing noise.

Clinks on her glass, again and again.

Anxiety is hanging around the room, watching my every move.

She drags the photo albums out from under the stairs, where she'd put them when Dad left, and she drops a big, heavy album, and photos of us all escape across the living room carpet.

Mum and me in the back garden.

Me and Nan in her kitchen – STRESS.

Toby standing on a swing at the park.

Dad playing a guitar, on the sofa.

Anxiety comes over and shoves me.

Bella sniffs at the pictures and follows Mum to the sofa as she goes through the pages of us all.

Normally she tries to get me to look at the old photos of Grandma and Uncle Pete, but she's lost in *her* own little world.

And I don't think that cheese sandwich is going to happen, so I go to the safety of my little pink room. With the hope that I can sneak away from Anxiety and leave it down here, but no such luck, it's right behind me as I lug the car crash and the moment of impact up the 12 steps. The moment of impact is still with me. There's no sneaking away. I can't sneak away from it.

I sit on the edge of my bed and try, try, try to shout out and release some of this tension, but nothing budges… No sound will come out.

The CRASH still in my body. I open my laptop. Documents and files of Lynx.

Lynx Lynx Lynx Lynx Lynx Lynx Lynx Lynx Lynx Lynx Lynx Lynx Lynx Lynx Lynx Lynx Lynx Lynx Lynx Lynx

No one knows about these files, on my home laptop.

I click on the file called "Lynx! Football in Tonbridge!" and see all the pictures of him smiling and arms around other football players, and in the background of another picture he is sleeping on the mini bus, and I click on another file I called "Lynx: Blue Hoodie."

His handsome face!

But then I think of the headmaster's office and the crash and these are bad things associated with Lynx. I click on YouTube and watch a scene from Skylar, season 5, episode 12. The episode is called "City of Dreams."

Skylar is on the balcony of a five-star Aphrodite penthouse suite in New York City. The sun is setting and a melody is forming. Skylar searches for an early evening star to connect with Ewan but instead sees a helicopter sweep past all the skyscrapers! It's Ewan! Ewan is the pilot and he waves at her, and the melody reaches a crescendo when they lock eyes, and high up over the City of Dreams he mouths, "I love you Sky!" And Skylar mouths back, "I love you too Ewan."

And I stop the clip at this point and watch the 1 minute 56 sec clip. Again. Again, my heart leaps and I get a rush of joy when Skylar realises Ewan's flown by from Chicago, Illinois, and that's 790 miles, on his way to Boston, Massachusetts – that's 215 miles before he plays a concert just to say, "I love you!" That's 1005 miles of love, love, love!

Again! The moment she realises he is the pilot!

Again! The moment he sees her wearing her satin, Japanese-style robe on the balcony.

Again! The moment the music changes from build-up to glorious melody!

Again! Again! These beautiful, life-enhancing moments! I already had 1078 views – now it is 1168 views.

Again! Ewan smiles and his blue eyes sparkle. 1216 views.

1293 views.

The clock on the corner of the screen is 1.48.

I stop the clip and the CRASH is still with me and I want it to go. Instinctively I go to the files marked Lynx. I open them and see the glorious array of pictures of Lynx. I really thought they were harmless.

I mean they are harmless. I notice that he has a green T-shirt on in five pictures, so I make The Green T-Shirt file. More of him, and that's a good thing! A pleasing thing! Isn't it? SIRENS blast through my head. Mr Crane said they were **against the law.** So this is the second criminal thing I've done today. The windscreen wipers and the Lynx files. What am I capable of? What law will I break next?

Criminal Criminal

wiper screeches

STALKING

sirens

POLICE

Excluded

Is it just a matter of time before I'm locked up in a cell or in court? I must be a terrible person. I don't even realise I'm breaking laws. I'm innately criminal.

I delete the files. All of them, and I don't love him any more. Love has brought too much trouble into my life. If I delete them then maybe some of this anxiety will get deleted with them.

DELETE DELETE DELETE DELETE DELETE DELETE DELETE DELETE DELETE DELETE DELETE DELETE

Bella noses the door open. I notice the room is white, lit by the moon. She looks at me and gives a low woof.

And I look at the screen again and see the final file… Lynx in Devon, Year 7. DELETE.

Bella nudges me with her big, wet Labrador nose. She wants to go outside and so do I.

★ ★ ★

"You need to go in M! M!" Dereck from next door is shouting but whispering over the garden fence. A very confusing tone. Is he angry? Is he warning me? Is he telling me because he cares?

The garden is alight glowing. Since I've been standing on the grass I've seen two cats pad by. They see me, stop and whizz off! And I've listened to the crows, high up in the trees, unsettled by the foxes screaming out. The garden and its delicate rhythms and patterns always soothes me. Toby just kicks a football around in the garden and never notices when he bashes a branch and disturbs a series of leaves and he skids on the grass, destroying nature's order.

"M, get in. It's three o'clock in the morning. Get inside and take that dog in with you," continues Dereck. I'd forgotten about Bella, standing front legs in the garden and back legs in the house. I turn and pat my thigh. Usually she runs up to me when I do that but she seems reluctant to leave her position. I think she wants to be a bit with me and a bit with Mum, in the house.

The systems in the garden always give me comfort because I too have systems and I am part of the system. And I think about Grandad as well and how he's part of all this too. Buried deep in the soil his decomposing body must have fed into the soil and that fed the trees, which oxygenate the air we breathe.

"M. Where is your mum?" I turn and look at Dereck, who is looking over the fence. "Get in. It's not right you being out here now. Go inside and turn the music off, it's too loud. I can't sleep. It's not safe you being out here." And he goes in.

But it's not safe inside either. Anxiety has been prowling and pouncing at me since we got in and tonight it feels merciless, but I follow Dereck's instructions and go in.

I sit at the end of the sofa and look at Mum. Bella puts her head on my knees and I stroke her soft head and she sighs. Usually Bella curls up on her rug in the night time but she's staying up and close with us tonight.

Mum looks so peaceful asleep and I wish I could find that peace, as the CRASH continues to smash through my brain and, still, I am in the moment of the collision.

And the stress in Mr Crane's office is still with me, layered on top of Mum shouting at me in the car. I wonder how I can get this all out of me. Through a cut or a scream? And I think can I cut this out of me? Like how we learnt in History, when they used to trepan people's heads. They'd drill a hole in their skull and let the pain out.

Will this end?

She's not sleeping straight. I try to straighten her neck and put a cushion under her head. Mum's favourite cushion that says, "Comfort and love make a home." Bella sniffs around Mum's face and knocks over two empty wine bottles. The clinks stab my head and disturb Mum a little, but she falls back into her sleep and I place a throw over her. It's a mohair blue and grey blanket she made and I tuck it in around her.

A hug.

It's the nearest I can get to hugging my mum. I watch her body rise and fall with her breathing. I follow her breathing and try to calm myself. Bella settles her head back on my knees.

And then I wonder, where is Toby? Is he in bed? I drag myself and the crash up the 12 stairs, Bella following me, and I edge open the door, half expecting him to shout,

"Go away you idiot!"

But he's not there. I don't like Toby very much and I hate his certificates, but I do love him and he should be in bed, and he said we would take Bella out this weekend, so where is he? His bedside clock says 4.58. I get myself across the landing to my little pink room. I get on to my bed and scrunch up in a little ball, pulling my blanket around me – tight.

Anxiety paces round my room and kicks at my bed and keeps a nasty, cruel presence in my room.

There is no order and I've been freefalling. Trying to put some sense to time and actions and activities, but nothing is right. The Beast has been very successful in his reign of terror tonight.

I am still in the moment of the CRASH and I can't get out of this moment.

Autism is a black, blue, red and yellow rainbow. Black is empty, blue is sad, red is angry and yellow is happy.

★ Chapter 20 ★

Jackie smells of blackcurrant sweets or chewing gum and cigarettes. She's currently sucking on a blackcurrant sweet and it clicks and clacks round her teeth. Strong, sweet and artificial, and she is sitting on the edge of my bed.

"What's been happening here, eh?"

I blink. 10.23.

"I believe you've stopped talking M?"

I must have fallen asleep. I am exhausted and still feeling like I'm in a collision. Scared and in shock. I see my laptop and instinctively I want to go to it. Watch Skylar.

"So I checked my phone this morning and there's a pissed-up message from your mum about the head at your school and it sounds like you're both having a party."

SILENCE

"It wasn't much of a party really, was it?"

I'm lost.

"I think it's all gone a bit off the rails here."

I'm really lost.

"I mean it's got in a bit of a mess. Home."

I could nod but I've given up having an opinion any more.

"It's not your fault M. You know that, don't you?"

I don't know that.

Toby! I jump up and look in his room. Where is he? Did he come home? I hate him but I love him, and I don't want any harm to come to him.

"He's at your dad's M."

And I breathe a sigh of relief. He is alive. I go towards my bedroom. My little sanctuary, but Jackie says to follow her.

I stand in the landing. Confused.

"Follow me. Just to the front garden."

And parked outside our little house is a yellow Beetle car.

"This is what the insurance company have given you." I step outside into the cool air and look at the bright, shiny car.

"Well, I say 'given.' They've lent it to you for a few weeks."

I run my hand over the bonnet. It's so pretty.

Yellow = happy. In Art we learnt that yellow is the first colour you see above all other colours. It is bright. It is bold. This car is just saying happiness.

"I believe you've got a week off M?"

I hang my head. I'm so ashamed of why I have a week off. I'm so stupid and I'm so sad at not realising it was such a terrible, terrible thing to do and I wonder if Jackie is going to tell me off.

"Well, you can't spend a week knocking about Sevenoaks, can you?"

Knocking about? I tilt my head slightly and Jackie adds,

"Hanging around doing sod all, which means doing nothing."

But I think the idea of doing nothing is a really good idea, if doing nothing means nothing will happen, including nothing bad.

"So, the cottage in Cornwall is free, so you and your mum are going to drive there and have a bit of a jolly. That means a holiday."

A holiday in term time? I tap my face.

"Let's go in and make a list. An order of events. A plan, M! Plus I think your mum needs to sober up before she gets behind the wheel of a car."

But I want to go to my room, so I go back to my sanctuary. Jackie follows me in and sits on the edge of my bed.

"You haven't done anything wrong M. I don't think you should have been excluded from school. Just 'cause he's the headmaster doesn't make him right, does it?"

"Doesn't it?" I think.

"And we all get bloody crushes."

CRUSH. I have been crushed.

"Even now M. I Googled some bloke from the accounts department at work the other day."

I look away. I feel ashamed.

"And I looked up Paul Jenkins from school the other day too."

I want to say, you didn't download 20,000 pictures of him.

"I ended up going through his wedding pictures on Facebook. We all do it."

And it doesn't really come close to what I did... And then Jackie adds,

"It's similar, isn't it? I think it comes from the same place...you know, within us, interested, attracted to someone. Wanting to get to know them."

Similar...maybe. I wanted to own him. Absorb Lynx into my cells. Did Jackie want that too?

"Mum said you're not seeing Fiona any more? Well, that's not going to help, is it?" And she clicks and clacks her blackcurrant sweet in and around her teeth. "It's a bloody nuisance really, isn't it? Fiona buggering off to have a baby?"

It is.

"And those girls at school sound horrid M. Nasty pieces of work. You need a bit of space from them."

I want permanent space from them. Already I am worrying about seeing them again. I tap my face.

"Do you know what I think, sweetheart? *They* should have been excluded. Not you."

And I look up at Jackie. She's right. They were the ones going through my bag. Pushing past me. Hurting me. Saying cruel things to me.

"I'd give you a big hug M but I know you don't like them. So have this, a virtual hug." And she kind of hugs the air.

She sucks on her sweet a bit more.

"And your mum. She's not really been…coping, has she?"

Cope.

"A little holiday will do you both a world of good."

A world of good.

And she takes some of my heart note paper.

"So you like a list don't you? It's your autism, isn't it M? You like a bit of order and that's great. You know where you are with a bit of order, don't you?" And it feel like ages since anyone has said autism in a good way. A nice way, like it's an OK thing to have. To be. She writes a list and says, "We'll go through it together."

1. Pack clothes.

2. Grey and purple blanket.

3. Red wellingtons.

4. Choose and pack toiletries.

5. Choose books.

6. Put in back of car.

7. Sleep.

8. Wake up.

9. Pack Bella.

10. GO to Cornwall.

Jackie doesn't say much and we spend the day working through the list.

Mum has a fridge magnet which reads,

BEST FRIENDS ARE PEOPLE WHO ARE ANGELS, WHO JUST FORGET TO PUT THEIR WINGS ON TODAY.

Maybe today Jackie is being like an angel. She takes in a cup of tea for Mum and wakes her up and helps her pack too. The house is quiet. They aren't singing or dancing like they usually do, or drinking more white wine and crying or being loud. I have to go up really close to the door to hear them talking, which is unusual as normally I'm telling them to be quiet.

"Thanks for this...for sorting the cottage out for us," says Mum.

"No problem."

SILENCE

And Jackie breaks it.

"I think it's time."

"Time?" replies Mum.

"To really face into things with M. She needs more…attention or support Mandy."

"I know…I know… She was doing so well with Fiona and she won't agree to talk to another counsellor, and then everything at school kicked off with that boy."

"Yeah… And this stuff with Simon… Can't be easy for her."

"I know. I know."

"It's a bloody mess, isn't it?"

"Yes, thank you Jackie."

"He's never going to be bloody Bono, is he?"

"I know! Why are you telling me all this?!"

"But it's like you're still hanging on a bit."

"He's my children's father. He will always be family. It's not hanging on."

"But it's like you haven't moved on completely… And you're dragging M…and Toby through…stuff!"

"Stuff?"

"Yeah…like you've got about 500 fridge magnets telling you how to breathe slowly and how 'to be the bloody change you want.'"

"Any more criticisms about my parenting? My marriage? My fridge magnets?"

"But it's like you've lost your way a bit…you're a bit…stuck."

STUCK STUCK STUCK

"Well, that's rich…says you with no children or a man in sight… Have you any idea how difficult this is?"

"Yes, Mandy, I do…that's exactly why I don't have any children or a man in sight."

"Well thanks! So me and my family put you off, did we? Thanks a million."

"Oh don't go all offended! I've seen you drink Snake Bite and vomit it up in a bucket."

"And what has this got to do with anything?"

"The point is, I've seen you in a few 'low' moments in life and you're still my best friend. I still care about you and I want what is best."

"You're not perfect Jackie."

"And my intention is not to criticise you… I've known M her whole life and I love her Mandy… It's *her* I am thinking about…surely it's my duty to speak up for her. I'm standing by and watching her suffer."

BIG SILENCE

Jackie breaks the silence again.

"I just don't think you can take your foot off the pedal when it comes to supporting M or working out what she needs, but you don't have to see everything as a fight or a battle or a criticism with M. It's not you against the world. Life isn't a series of winning and losing."

"I'm just tired."

"You would be. You've taken the world on and all on your own."

SILENCE

Mum breaks the silence.

"Yeah…"

"Just let your guard down a bit. Just be you. Not super mum. Be the Amanda I knew at university… maybe without the Snake Bite and vomiting in a bucket."

"Yeah… I prefer Chardonnay these days."

"And one more thing…"

"Yes?"

"Please, get rid of that fridge magnet that says,

WOMEN ARE LIKE TEABAGS, YOU NEVER
KNOW HOW STRONG THEY ARE TILL
YOU PUT THEM IN HOT WATER.

I'm not a teabag Amanda."

And my mum starts to laugh. And I don't understand why she is laughing, because Jackie has made a very valid point and I totally agree with Jackie, who goes on to say,

"I've always hated it and you're not a teabag either! But you are strong and I just think you have to continue being strong. But it isn't about fighting everything or trying to force things to work. Be a bit kinder to yourself…gentler. Go and have this holiday and let things just…be."

In my head I agree and I think she can tell.

"Years for the doctors to believe me that you were struggling and felt things…differently, and that day in the hospital when they gave us the results it was like travel away from St. Andrew's and the stupid things I did there, the more relaxed I become.

People are beeping us as we drive along the

beige speckles and she's standing in the corner of the field.

Turned away from us.

"I got her dinner here." And he holds up a metal bucket and shakes it, loudly. "Let's go see if she'll eat." We walk towards her and I see her back legs shake, and she trots away and puts distance between us. A safe distance. Paul shakes the bucket again, her trot speeds up and she moves further away, but always keeping to the edge of the field.

"Most animals come to me when I have food. See? She's not right." He empties the bucket of grains and apples on to the ground. We take a few steps back and slowly, warily, she walks towards her food. She sniffs, chews, crunches. All the time, watching us.

"She doesn't like people, so what am I supposed to do with her?"

And I think I understand that, Marigold.

"No! Can't afford to keep her." She stops eating and jolts back to the corner. "Marigold. Come here," he demands. She doesn't. I walk towards her. Keeping lots of space between us, I look into her big, dark, glassy eyes. She is scared. I can see her fear.

"Keep your distance M. She's a kicker and I don't fancy a trip to Penzance Emergency Department this afternoon." Paul's wife, Laura, enters the field and Marigold pushes herself further into the corner.

"M!" Laura shouts out as she walks towards us. "How are you? We don't normally see you this time of year. Is everything all right?"

I remain silent.

"M's not talking Laura. She's just giving me lots of looks."

"Don't blame you M, talking causes trouble half the time, doesn't it?"

And I think "half the time" would be good. Talking causes me trouble *all* the time.

"Bet you like Marigold?" says Laura. "We've only had her a month and Paul wants rid of her."

And I wonder where has Marigold been? What terrible changes has she been through? And she probably *needs* secure little corners of the field. Like my little pink room at home. A little piece of safety in the big, wide world. Marigold needs a chance to get used to her new home. Maybe she can hear and feel that Paul doesn't want to keep her and isn't giving her a chance. So how *can* she get used to her home?

Mum enters the field and, again, Marigold is unsettled and kicks and snorts and pushes herself into the corner further, and I know what she's saying, she's saying, "Go away and leave me alone." The adults greet each other. Normally, Mum whoops and waves when she sees Paul and Laura. Instead she wanders quietly and they all hug. Laura asks if everything's OK and Mum says,

"We've had a tough couple of months. So we're having a little break."

Some summers Mum and Laura have stood talking in this field till night time. I think this must mean they are good friends because they "enjoy spending time together and the conversation flows" (from "How To Tell If She's A Real Friend," *Cherry Magazine*, The Friendship Special). Mum is very good at making friends and keeping friends. I am not.

And it's different in February. The air is cold and icy. Wind blasts into our faces and shakes at my yellow kagool. The ground is hard mud, with patches of grass, which are a deeper, darker green. And it smells so good! So fresh and clean, and I draw the cold air, deep, deep into my lungs.

Night arrives much earlier too and the dark is different to August dark. We've only been here one night but I can feel the February nights are blacker, denser. I like them.

I watch Marigold. She is watching us. I pick some of the grains and apples she has left on the ground, hold them out in my hand and walk towards her. She freezes. I go a little nearer and then Paul shouts,

"Careful M. Don't walk anywhere near her back legs. She'll kick you. She's a kicker. She's skittish."

Marigold bolts.

"See! Skittish, and that is a big problem." And I can see that it's us who are making her jump and kick and now she's been given that label, a problem. "And you try getting her in the stable every night, takes too long. She'll have to go. I'm a farmer, not an animal rescue centre, and stop looking at me like that M." Paul exits the field and, just like the school gates, the gate CLANGS shut and the CLANG goes through me, and again Marigold's body shakes and she kicks out her back legs. Paul shouts, "If you can calm her M, I might be able to keep her, but otherwise she's down the auction."

Mum and Laura are still talking, and at one point Laura gives Mum a b-i-g H-ug.

The hug unsettles me. I breathe in the cold, winter air and stand facing Marigold.

She swishes her tail.

Gently, I hold out an apple for her.

She sniffs the air.

Mum and Laura are still standing in the field talking.

The sunlight is fading.

Marigold steps towards me and throws her head and mane back.

I stand still and in a quiet voice I tell her she is beautiful and safe.

Marigold steps nearer and snorts and, again, swishes her tail.

I keep whispering and tell her,

"It's OK."

And I realise it's dark and the field is being lit by some lights from the farm house.

I stand still and I lower my eyes. She steps forward, sniffing, sniffing the air.

Mum and Laura watching me.

She snorts and slowly, slowly, Marigold reaches her neck out towards me and takes the apple. She withdraws a little as her big teeth crunch it. Still she watches me and takes a few steps back.

And I don't know how long it took for Marigold to calm and trust me...but she did. It may have been an hour or two hours, but it felt like time very well spent.

★ ★ ★

After dinner Mum and I sit by the log fire. Bella is lying on a tatty, faded rug, loving the heat. Content and relaxed. Not like three nights ago when Mum drank all that wine. Bella was so unsettled…we all were. I love that Bella is peaceful now. That is what I want for her because I know that, when peace arrives, it is the best feeling in the world.

I stare into the flames and enjoy the heat. I feel calm and realise this is the first time I have been relaxed for…I just don't know how long…months?

The cottage has little, swirly draughts blowing through it in February. The air that sweeps in from the Atlantic that travels from America and the Caribbean Islands, then blows through the cracks in the windows and swirls around the cottage! And it feels cosier and smaller in the winter. The doors and windows are shut, but I feel more aware of the elements as the wind blows and the fire burns! More alive! Connected up, in the great system of life. The fire **cracks**! Bella raises her head and looks into the flames, briefly. Reassured, she rests her head back on the tatty rug and back into her deep slumber.

Mum is curled up on the big, fraying sofa, reading. She is biting her finger nails and is very engrossed in the story. I go through the pile of books I brought.

I rush up to my room. I don't want to go back to that school! I can't go back there! And I lie on my little bed and wrap my blanket around me, tightly.

And it's Monday night and the little square of timetable time states that I should be packing my school bag for Geography and Maths, tomorrow morning! But I don't want to be at that school any more.

Mum enters.

"Look, to be honest I don't want you to go back there either, but I just don't know what to do and you were doing well at St. Andrew's once…and your big brother is there and that should be a good thing! It just seems that we shouldn't give up! Shouldn't give into the bullies!"

And this is NOT about giving up. She doesn't understand. This is about survival.

"I know I am a mother and I should have all the answers, but I don't know what to do."

Bella barges in and the three of us are in my little bedroom just like in Sevenoaks, and we've driven hundreds of miles for hours and hours and it turns out I brought all my problems with me, and of course The Beast of Anxiety has pursued me to Cornwall and up the stairs and is now prowling about the landing and I breathe deeply to keep it at bay. To keep it away from me.

And I realise there is no holiday from autism.

There is no escape.

Autism is not
a disease, it is simply
just a special need.

★ Chapter 23 ★

WELCOME TO ZENNOR COVE

Z. Zennor. Z – I like Z. Zennor.

Mum and I are walking to Zennor Cove. It's very near the cottage and there is a little café there too, so we can eat cake and then go to the beach. I love the beach and I love cake. I am wearing a stripy blue and white T-shirt, blue skinny jeans and my yellow rain jacket. This is the same outfit that Skylar wore when she went sailing in season 8, episode 8, "All Aboard!" When she sailed around the South of France, with a record producer, called LP Addison, who tried to lure her away from Ewan! I am wearing red wellies though. I have never seen Skylar wear a wellington boot.

The 9-Point Plan was on the kitchen table this morning, when I came down for breakfast. Waiting for me. I kept my head down as I ate my cereal and I wouldn't look at it.

I can't sign it. I can't agree to it.

Mr Crane's signature:

Mr M.J. Crane

There on the kitchen table. A part of him here. I don't like it.

And I am full of relief when Mum says,

"Come on, let's go for a walk." Bella barks with excitement.

Zennor. Z – I like Z. Zennor.

Zennor Cove is one of the best places in the universe. I think it's better than The Rockefeller Center, New York City, which Skylar visits in season 8, episode 1. She has champagne on the roof terrace and says, "NYC. The best place in the Universe!" But actually, in this case, I don't think she is right. She might change her mind about that if she visited Zennor Cove.

Bella is pulling, pulling, pulling at the lead as we walk along the quiet road to Zennor Cove.

I clap my hands.

Z Z Z Z. It's a much better letter than M. It's not stuck in the middle of the alphabet being shoved and jostled and pushed about by all the other letters.

It Zings and it's Zappy – I think the letter Z has places to go...to whiZZZZZZZ off to. Plus I think it has friends too. X and Y. Who are quite cool. And maybe they are at the end because they aren't used as much as the other letters, so they just hang out down the end of the alphabet, relaxing and not stressing out about being included. I like Z.

I smile to myself and let out a squeal of happiness. Sometimes I really like being me. Mum asks,

"What's so funny M?"

And I say,

"ZZZZZZennor," and Mum giggles and says,

"Good to hear your voice."

★ ★ ★

The fluorescent light in the café is buzzing. The smell of baking is sweet and warm, but they've just mopped the floor, so the stink of disinfectant is strong in the air, getting into my respiratory system, and I can taste the fake pine. Unpleasant chemicals. I feel poisoned.

M in Mocha

M in Milk shake

M in Mint tea

M in LeMon DriZZle

A thin, loud tinny sound is coming from the little radio by the till, which BEEPS as the woman presses the buttons. A loud heater, attached to the ceiling, pumps out sickly, hot air. As is so common in my life, I want to stay but I want to go. I want to stay and finish my Red Velvet cake, but I want to go and get some fresh air into my lungs. Bella is watching me eat cake and is slobbering.

Usually at this point Mum would be planning and fussing and organising and insisting I have a glass of water or arranging "fun games" on the beach or "a nice picnic" or trips to "an interesting botanical garden." And sometimes I try to block her plans or throw them aside or run away from them and disappear into MOLW or my little pink bedroom, but sometimes I just can't! And the PLANS and DREAMS and FUSS weigh me down...

PLANS
DREAMS
FUSS

And they
   layer
   layer
   layer
   layer

on to all my other worries.

And I think all her planning and fussing are *her* worries in disguise. Disguised as care or love or concern, and she layers them on top of me, and I just don't know where to put them…so I carry them around. Lug them upstairs, drag them to school, and haul them around corridors and classrooms… But right now, she has stopped. And I enjoy her peace and the peace it brings me.

And I then hear a sound that is unmistakable.

And I look over.

And the sound.

Unmistakable.

"Nooooooo."

Mum stops and listens too.

Mum puts down her coffee cup and turns her head to look at the man and girl sat at the table by the door.

My whole world **ZOOMS** into the sound and the tension and the stress. And I have never seen this before, not in real life. I've seen pictures in leaflets or on the internet but never in real life. And this isn't good but I am amazed. This isn't good but my whole world

expaaaaaaaannnnnnnddddddssss

and I hear the man say,

"You do need to eat something."

"I doooooont want to!"

This is someone's misfortune but I understand what is going on. I know and I *never* know. I am always the one on the edge – not knowing. But I understand what is happening.

The girl is struggling. Tears drop one after the other after the other.

And the man, who must be her dad, says,

"OK then, let's go outside. Get some air."

She is shaking and her face is red and she pushes the word out,

"Noooooo."

And I know she does want to get out but she can't! I know! She is trapped. Perhaps she doesn't want to walk past that grinding electric heater pumping out that nasty hot air. Maybe the electronic beeps of the till are slicing through her head and Anxiety is pinning her to the chair. She's trapped by her body and mind.

I am looking in at me.

I stand up and open the café door and let the cold air swirl in and travel to her, and when it arrives to her I see her calm a little, and it's as if an escape route opens up for her and she rushes outside. The man follows and slowly I do too. I step outside the café and watch as he tells her to do her coat up. Mum comes out.

"Everything all right?"

And the man says,

"Sorry if we've disrupted your coffee. She's not feeling too good today and thanks for letting some air in. Got a bit stuffy for Jess in there."

And she looks up at me with her terrified eyes and she says,

"Thank you."

And I want to say "thank you" to her because even if it's just for two or three minutes of my life I've met someone who is going through what I go through! I am not alone.

"She hasn't disrupted us at all," replies Mum, and adds, "Are...are you OK?"

The girl's eyes dart to the ground. Of course she's not OK. How could Mum ask such a stupid question?

"Not been a great day, has it Jess?" says the man. "We had a massive meltdown this morning and then something in the café tipped her right back into another."

And my mum keeps repeating the word "right." "Right...right... A meltdown?"

"Jess is on the autistic spectrum, so we have meltdowns on a regular basis... I'm not sure what that was about though. Was it that radio Jess?"

"Nooo. The out-of-date food. All the dates on the muffins by the till are wrong. They said use by the 3rd and today is the 4th."

"I didn't notice," he says, and then explains, "Dates are very important to Jess. To be honest we usually get disapproving looks from holiday makers in cafés, don't we Jess? So thanks for asking if we're OK! Makes a change!" Is Mum going to tell them about me? She just keeps saying, "Right...right...." Like she is trying to work something out or understand something.

"Are you autistic?" Jess asks.

How could she tell? Do I look it?

"Jess is direct," says her dad.

I nod.

And the dad throws his hands in the air and says,

"Well, you know exactly what our mornings have been like then, don't you? Jess had a bad few days, her anxiety has been through the roof, so I decided to take her out of school today and go to the beach... It often helps calm her down."

"Right," says Mum again.

"But turns out a slice of carrot cake in a café with out-of-date muffins didn't help!"

And I totally understand that. Something is NOT as it should be!

Jess is already walking towards the beach. Her shoulders are hunched and I recognise the weakness you feel after a meltdown. Life and energy are taken away from you and you are left spent.

"Hang on Jess!" shouts her dad as he walks after her. "You joining us?" he calls back. "Come on, it's a glorious morning."

★ ★ ★

Mum and Jess's dad walk ahead of us on the beach.

Bella is dragging a massive piece of driftwood along the sand and trying to get us to throw it for her.

Mum is nodding lots and really listening to Jess's dad. Again, Mum connecting and making friends… so easily.

The wind blows cold and hard, and it turns and *swirls* the opal and blue sea. And I swear it looks like there are white lights in the waves, and the swirls are the same shape as the draughts in the cottage, only much bigger! The same swirls in the night sky of the Van Gogh painting! Nature dancing! And I think how I have never been anywhere as magnificent as Zennor Cove. The hushing of the sea calms me and connects me to the moon and the tides and the planets. Life on this earth makes more sense when I walk on the beach.

And here I am, walking along the shore with someone who I understand and connect with.

"Why aren't you at school?" asks Jess. I look into the horizon... Do I have to explain...?

"Is it the same reason as me?" she asks. I shrug my shoulders. Jess has already told me that her parents are divorced and her mum's just had a baby, Bluebell, with her new husband, Josh Farley, and further explains,

"My dad says Josh Farley is too young for her, but I don't care what age he is because I just don't like him. He's always telling me to 'lighten up' or 'stop being so annoying.' I was visiting at the weekend and I said Bluebell might be like me, autistic, because sometimes it is inherited within families, and he got really, really annoyed and then he took me home, one day early. It was actually very humiliating."

I nod. I understand humiliation.

"And I said, 'What's wrong with being autistic anyway, Josh Farley?' And he said my mum doesn't want to hear it because she wants a normal family life now."

Normal.

"Poor Bluebell, I think Josh would be a very difficult Daddy."

I nod.

"I was only telling the truth, which everyone instructs me to do, but then, when I deliver honesty, it makes people angry. What's your name?" asks Jess.

And I grab a big pebble and in the sand I write…M.

"Are you really called Emma?"

I shake my head.

"My name is M," I say.

"M?"

"Yes."

"Is that what your mum and dad named you? It's a very unusual name. In fact, it's a bit odd."

"I chose it."

"You chose your own name? Can you do that?"

"Well I did!"

"Does it mean anything?"

I nod and tell her about the long, alphabet poster stuck round the edges of the classroom, in Year 3. A is for apple and D is for dancer, and in the middle was M, and that's just always how I felt. M in the Middle.

"Wow!!!! That is sooooo cool!" says Jess, but I tell her it wasn't really that cool because, as I explain,

"I had this horrible teacher who was always shouting at me and telling me to '*Focus! FOCUS!*' and '*Stop fidgeting!*' – so to escape from her impatience and picking on me I just stared at the beautiful long lines and its pleasing symmetry, but still it was stuck in the middle. Can't get out. Trapped."

"I want a name!" she yells and claps her hands. "That's just so cool. I want a new name, like you!" And then she says something I've never heard in my whole life. She says, "I want to be like you M."

I want to be like you M.

Someone wants to be like me!?

We stand by the giant M. I am utterly amazed and the sentence boings around my head.

And the vast sound of the sea, so broad and magnificent, fills me, *and* I am full of good words and good sounds. I am glad to be alive.

And I think about last week in the library and I thought I'd never fit in, and I looked at *Our Solar System* and how it said that Planet Earth is the fifth biggest planet in the solar system, with a diameter of

8000 miles, that it's 4.5 billion years old and spins on its axis every 23 hours and 56 minutes and has a liquid metal inner core that's hotter than the surface of the sun, and I worried I'd never find a place for myself on this planet, but I have! I do fit in. I fit in here in Zennor Cove.

Breathe in.

Breathe out.

And I hear Jess shout out,

"I've found my new name M!" And she's looking up to the white and grey billowing clouds and she shouts,

"Sky!"

I too look up into the clouds. They are clearing and the sun is now big and bold in the sky!

"Because I am like the sky!" she continues. "Detached from this earth. A huge distance between me and everyone else, but looking in at people and their lives, but there's no way I can ever be with them or they can be with me or hold or contain me. I'm very separate from them."

And I clap my hands! I totally understand!

"Are we friends?" she asks.

"Yes," I reply. "I'd love that more than anything in this big, wide vast universe!"

Autism is my chance to shine. I have an opportunity to be different and unique.

★ Chapter 24 ★

"Is this what he looks like?" We sit at the kitchen table and Sky sketches lots of the things and people as I tell her about my life, in response to her direct questions! She does ask *lots* of direct questions...

Mum and Sky's dad, who is called Adam, are in the lounge area and her dad keeps shouting over to her,

"Make sure you're having a conversation. Remember what we discussed and don't ask too many questions – people don't like it!"

And Sky says,

"OK Daddy."

And she turns to me and asks,

"Do you have a boyfriend M?"

But I like her direct questions.

After the walk on the beach Mum invited Adam and Sky in for a cup of tea and Adam said he could go through some of the things he'd learnt and the many mistakes he'd made while trying to get his daughter into the right school and work out what she was entitled to.

I'd hoped he wouldn't bring too many of his mistakes into the cottage.

"Is Joe handsome?" asks Sky.

"Err…I guess. He's nice."

"But he's definitely not your boyfriend?"

"No," I reply. "He has a floppy fringe though," I say, and she makes some changes to the drawing.

"You're so lucky, M. I wish I had a friend who was a boy…it's just so cool."

And I hope he will still want to be my friend. I hope he didn't get scared about all the pictures of Lynx and think "Shaznia was right, you are weird." I hope I haven't ruined my friendship with Joe too.

"Can't he be your boyfriend?"

"I don't want a boyfriend… Not at the moment."

"I'd love a boyfriend. There's this boy at school called Tyler and we went on a date to 'Blue Dreams' café for hot chocolate and it was OK. I asked, 'Are you my boyfriend Tyler?' and he said, 'No,' so I was hurt but the date was OK."

"Just OK?"

"Yes, but just OK is good! Dad says that all the time. He says OK is a good feeling. Not too high and not too low. Not too anxious and not too exhausted."

OK OK OK OK

And I think about how much I loved Lynx and how I wanted more than OK. Maybe I should have just stuck with feeling OK. Maybe I should text Joe. Say hello, and I think about how Joe always said he likes coming to visit me and he liked my family. I don't think I ever really believed him.

★ ★ ★

Mum is curled up on the big, faded chair and Adam is sitting on the sofa looking at the internet. Which is where Dad sat when he used to come to Cornwall. And I hear Mum say to Adam, in a low, quiet but perfectly audible whisper,

"I can't believe M's speaking. This is wonderful."

"She's lucky she can get a word in with Jess… sorry Sky."

"She must be feeling so much happier. Your daughter is really helping M. I was beginning to wonder if she'd ever speak again."

"Like I say, not really a worry I've ever had with Jess. She just tells me her feelings and thoughts as they arrive to her! I know where I stand with her!"

Adam is also writing down a list and I can hear words and letters rise up from them.

Statement
DLA
Evidence
PIP
Waiting List
Panel Process
Special Needs School
Social Worker
SEN
Case Officer
OCD
CBT
Exam Concession
Education, Health and Care Plan

* * *

"I have this planet," says Sky, drawing a library book, "where I go sometimes and it's called PRA. The People's Republic of Autism, and it has only autistic people living on it. And it is as far away, as possible, from the Earth."

"Further than Neptune?" I ask.

"Yes! And no NTs live there!"

"NTs?"

"Like those two over there." And she points to Mum and Adam. "Neuro-Typical. Those that are not on the spectrum, those that are normal, allegedly… everyone else. The others."

"NTs?" And I think, there is a word for them!?

"The ones on the other side of the pane of glass."

And I know exactly what she means.

"In PRA people say what they mean and give clear instructions!" And I tell her about MOLW and the beautiful mountain ranges I escape to and she repeats,

"MOLW! Wow!"

"It's only me in MOLW. No one else, so there is never any pressure."

"There are no bullies in PRA!" adds Sky.

And Nev and Lara and Shaznia and What I Did crashes into my head and rattles at my peace. I shake my head to try and get rid of them. I don't want them here.

"In PRA I fit in all the time and I don't have to hide anything about me! What's your thing M?"

"Thing?"

"Other than Lynx, because to be honest he did sound like a *special interest* to me. I like dates and times and love to draw. I like to draw events and things and people, even though people are always shocked when they discover an autistic person is creative. My school want me to do GCSE Art and Drama a year early."

Special interest?

"I love Art too and I like the letter M. Does that count? I like to find M when I feel anxious or sometimes just because it is a nice thing to do, pleasing. I love clothes and make-up. I do watch a lot of Skylar... Mum says I watch too much." And maybe Lynx was my thing, and I feel stupid and it hurts and I want to put it in the past. Delete it, but I'm not sure I can delete it from Shaznia and Nev and Lara's mind.

"Oh my God! There's this girl at my school and she loves Skylar too and she is also totally obsessed with cats! My other thing is I like property prices. Where do you live?"

"Sevenoaks. In Kent. Really near London."

"That is super expensive, for properties. You get much more space for your money in Cornwall. You should come and live here!" And I think how brilliant that would be because we'd live by the sea, but mostly it would be brilliant because I wouldn't have to return to St. Andrew's.

"We'll have to Skype and email to maintain our friendship because Sevenoaks is not an easy destination for me to get to."

She wants to "maintain" our friendship!

"So what do I draw next?" asks Sky. "What next shall I draw from Marvellous M from Sevenoaks' life? I know, I'll draw the yellow car and the steps up to your nan's flat in The Oval."

She's really listened to everything I've said. I examine the picture of the two empty bottles of wine that Mum drank a few nights ago and I think it's really not in The Card Emporium series of life events, is it…?

★ ★ ★

More familiar words rise from the two NTs on the sofa.

Simon
Toby
Art School
Jackie
Sofa Simon
Separation

Textiles
Work
Simon's band
Bluebell
Normal family life
Josh Farley
Jessie's mum

✿ ✿ ✿

"Do you have to go back to that school M? It sounds awful," Sky says.

"I am thinking that if my mum makes me I will have to sit in a café or travel round on the aisle seat of a bus all day or sneak back home when she's at work."

"That sounds soooo stressful."

"Maybe I might run away."

"But that's too dangerous."

"What could be more dangerous than that school, those people? They want me to sign this plan. A 9-Point Plan, but I can't."

I breathe in deeply and I hand the 9-Point Plan to Sky. She reads and then says,

"Sooooo Neuro-Typical. 'Point number 1. On return to school the student is required to talk to an appropriate member of staff for support, when required, e.g. Head of Pastoral Care.' But you've already told me you can't speak when you are stressed! I can't believe it! You should write your own M!" And I think what my 9-Point Plan would be…

Sky draws Bella, and I tell her more about the library and how kind the librarian was and I think how this room feels OK. Five of us in this room and we are all OK. I don't think there is a Card Emporium card that reads,

"Well done! You are OK!"

OK is a good way to be. A good thing to feel. And maybe that's enough to feel in life?

I'm OK because I have a friend. A girl friend, and we've talked about boys and our parents, and like it says in *Cherry Magazine*, The Friendship Special, "How To Tell If She's A Real Friend":

You have a fab girlfriend if you feel comfortable telling her about your life – the good and not so good. Lucky you! Why not share an important part of your life! Introduce them to another friend or tell them about a special achievement that you are very proud of!

"Come with me," I say. "I want you to meet Marigold."

"I can't hear when you mumble M."

"She's absolutely not mumbling," says Sky. "I think you have partial hearing loss Paul." Sky and I are standing in the field with Paul, Laura and Marigold. Marigold has already eaten two carrots and an apple from my hand. Laura is laughing.

"That's what I've been saying for years! He is as deaf as a post."

"A post?" I question.

"Yeah, deaf like a piece of wood…just deaf! He's deaf!"

"What?" says Paul.

"You're deaf Paul. Deaf!" Paul's face is very difficult to understand. I examine his eyes, which have become slits. I hope he's not cross.

"But don't worry Paul," says Sky, "because there is a boy in my school with partial hearing like you, and he wears hearing aids that work very well. I suspect your deafness is age related though, as you are old." Paul folds his arms, bites his lip and nods. Sky continues, "To be honest, Paul, if I were Marigold I'd be scared of you too."

Laura is giggling.

"So M, before your new friend here…"

"Sky, my name is Sky."

And Paul continues,

"...Sky, informed me that I am deaf and old, you were saying something?"

"You said you'd give Marigold a chance...if I calmed her."

"So yesterday, M, you wouldn't even talk and, today, you are telling me how to manage my farm."

"I'm not telling you how to manage the farm but you did say you'd consider keeping her."

"You did Paul, and it's very important you keep your word," adds Laura.

"But it's all very well, you giving her an apple, but if she doesn't respond to me, it's no good. I'm not sure keeping her will work."

"And what the girls are trying to explain to you is that it's because you shout!" says Laura.

"The sheep over there don't think I shout. They come over and get their food."

"Just try...whispering...to start with," I say and hand him an apple.

"Go on Paul," says Laura.

"I'm NOT whispering to a bloody farm animal!" he shouts, and Marigold takes a few steps back. "This is a farm, not a bloody Disney film. A working farm."

"The high volume of your voice just caused her to back away. It's you she is scared of. Can't you see the direct link?" says Sky.

"Farms are not places for the faint hearted. We buy and sell animals. They're our stock. If an animal isn't fitting in or working for me, I sell them on, and that's how I have been running this farm for over 40 years."

"Maybe it's time to learn something new then and stop being a contrary sod. Try Paul, and you never know it might work and end up being good for business!" Paul holds the apple out to her.

"Whisper to her," I say.

"I don't know what to say to a pony."

"Well say nothing then," I suggest. "Just be… calm." And we all watch as Marigold sniffs the air and slowly, slowly walks towards the apple in Paul's outreached hand. And Paul is calmer. I sense it too. He's stopped talking and shouting and fussing and he's giving Marigold some space to trust and be herself… so, of course, she takes the apple! And I think Paul is really pleased and I don't cheer, even though I really, really want to, because I want to keep building on Marigold's trust, but I clap my hands. Marigold trots off.

"Well, you two seem to know so much about farming, perhaps you'd like to fix the tractor door and lamb a few sheep."

"He's joking," Laura says to us both.

"I understand that," says Sky. "I may be autistic but I do have a sense of humour. It just wasn't very funny."

Laura laughs, a lot.

★ ★ ★

We go back into the cottage and Mum and Adam are still talking.

"Dad, we just saw this amazing horse which M has tamed, and do you fancy M's mum?"

"Yeah, all right Jess, we're going in 15 minutes. So finish off your drawings."

"But do you?"

"Inappropriate. Go and sit down."

Does he? Does my mum fancy Adam? He didn't say "No" and they are talking a lot, which, according to *Cherry Magazine*, The Flirt Issue, means:

This friendship is hotting up to a relationship and could be soaring from zero to a sizzling 10.

Oh GOD!!!! No! And I CRinge! And I think about Dad and I really want to see my dad. I want to walk around the block with him and Bella. Is Dad getting SHOVED and pushed out of the family?

Me and Sky sit down at the table and I watch her draw as I listen to Adam.

★ ★ ★

"I wish I'd had someone to explain to me! To show me it was all going to be OK...most of the time. 'Cause let's be honest, the meltdowns keep on melting down, the anxiety keeps on attacking, but that's the way our gorgeous daughters are and it's about helping them manage."

And Mum talks in a hushed voice...which always makes me want to listen more...

"It's caused a lot of stress with the family..."

"Tell me about it..."

"And that makes me feel so guilty to say...Toby, well, he is never in because it's...so stressful at home and he's such a great kid, a really high achiever, but I really understand because I want to run away too and then the guilt kicks in, big time, and it feels like I'm always letting one child down...or both!"

"Oh yes, guilt! Hello guilt, would you like to meet stress and would you like to meet another one of my constant companions, frustration."

And Mum is laughing and she adds,

"And frustration would you like to meet confusion, it's accompanied me throughout most of my parenting?"

Adam laughs too. I like Adam.

✱ ✱ ✱

Sky shows me some letters she has been writing:

AFF

"What does that mean?" I ask.

"Autistic Friends Forever!"

"WOW!"

✱ ✱ ✱

And they are still talking in hushed voices, like we can't hear. But I can hear…

"I think what I have learnt is that life is a series of stages," says Adam.

And I think…oh no, we're not going into fridge magnet territory, are we?

"You never know what the next stage will be... It might be the end of your marriage...or a new relationship...a new friendship...a new job...a new house...and Jessica...or should I say Sky...is part of all that... She just rolls with it all... It's family life. It's *my* family life. And of course I worry. I worry about what will happen after school, what boys she will meet! God, do I worry about boys! But then I know there is no point. We can only worry about so much. Walks on the beach tend to sort a lot of our bad days and problems out. I mean would Claire have run off with the local crystal healer if Jess was autistic or not?"

"Crystal healer?"

"Yeah...and he had the nerve to come round with some quartz and tell me to place them under Jess's pillow. To rebalance her chakra and create a more balanced aura around her."

"Seriously?" says Mum. "What did you do?"

"I walked him off my premises and used a few words that he said offended his energy and discovered that quartz, when thrown at a moving BMW, causes a really big dent."

BMW

And I say to Sky,

"We've both got broken families?"

And she stops drawing and says,

"No! My family is blended! Dad won't let me use that word. He says Mum hasn't broken off and neither has Bluebell, and when you think about it you can't really break a family, can you? You might not see someone for days or years but they are still family. Whether you like it or not!"

And she starts a new picture.

✻ ✻ ✻

I listen back to Adam saying,

"Yeah, now she's with Josh, all of 22 years old… bit of an idiot really. Hot headed. I don't want Jess going round there, but what can I do? She wants to see her new baby sister and Claire is her mother."

"You just want to protect them…it kills me when I think about some of the situations she might get in to…well, that she's already got into…"

"But I do believe it's better than pretending. I still love Claire and her flighty ways, but she was always running away from Jess and her autism."

"Me too… I've remained present in M's life but recently I've not given her the attention she needs… I've been 'willing' things to be better, plus trying to get on with work and everyday life."

"Maybe one day Claire will realise that Jess is Jess, our beautiful daughter…or should I say Sky…because I genuinely don't think that until you finally grasp autism, welcome it, include and embrace autism in your family, do you ever get *some* peace. When you stop trying to cure it or ignore it and realise that it's brilliant too! And that there are really difficult days as we grapple with and try to understand it, but who the bloody hell are we to judge anyway? It is what it is! We are who we are!"

SILENCE

"Just a few pearls of wisdom that I've learnt… Don't mean to give you a lecture… Claire always said I went on too much, but I just wish I'd known all this earlier. It might help you…" Mum nods and says,

"Acceptance."

"Yeah…accepting autism in all its magnificent, difficult, fantastic glory and living alongside it, with it, around it!"

And Mum cries. Not like the Jackie and white wine tears or the tears in the car when we crashed. These are different tears because she is laughing too, which is very confusing, and I don't know how they fit in the tear chart I created in the New Forest, when her tears went "off the scale." And I sooo want to give her a big hug, but it's just something I cannot do – in all my magnificent, difficult, fantastic glory.

★ ★ ★

Sky shows me her picture. And it's me, Mum, Dad, Toby, Bella, Grandad, Grandma and Nan, and next door is her and her dad and a cat. And next door to them is her mum and Josh Farley and Bluebell.

We're not broken families! Just not all living in the same house!

I'm not weird. I'm awesome.

★ Chapter 25 ★

"Come on M, it's time for bed. What are you writing?" asks Mum. I curl my legs up on the sofa. I haven't finished yet. Bella is still stretched out in front of the fire...which is burning low. The heat is dropping and I can feel the swirly draughts fly through the room.

Sky and Adam left exactly 15 minutes after he said, which was very reassuring and made me like him more. And I think about these two people who have entered our lives and how my world has now shifted on its axis. The world seems different. At a different angle.

"I spoke to Toby earlier. Sounds like him and your dad have been having a good time. Your dad's been staying at ours and he said Toby and he watched a film last night...and he stayed in last night. We need to watch a few films in...together...a lot more."

I keep writing.

"It's been fun meeting Jess – Sky… Hasn't it?"

And I think it's been more than fun. I feel as though I've been shelved in the right place in the library! And it's great being in the right place.

"We thought we could all meet up and have another walk, before we go back."

And I don't want to go back.

"Adam was telling me all about Sky and she's very different to you M, but she's very similar in lots of ways too. She can't really feel the cold and she's really messy – not like you…and she likes hugs."

Hugs

And the word hangs in the air.

"He said there is this saying and it goes, 'If you've met one autistic girl, you've met one autistic girl.'"

And I just think I am delighted to have met one autistic girl.

I hand Mum my sheet of paper.

M's 9-Point Plan

1. If what I am doing is right for me, then don't judge me or make me change my mind.

2. Don't say, "Don't get anxious."

3. If something feels wrong to me then respect it!

4. Be patient. I'll get there eventually.

5. Don't ask too many questions.

6. Let me create and live in good order.

7. Create proper timings and keep to them.

8. No changing plans at the last minute – without explaining fully.

9. When explaining something – always give your actual reasons. Don't say something, just because it's easier.

Mum reads and nods.

"Wow."

"I want to go to a school like Sky. They let her have time out and then you can learn, and they actually *believe* she has autism."

"She's happy there, isn't she?"

"And there are other *girls* with autism too."

"A *special* school though M?"

"I just want to go somewhere where I can be me!"

Mum takes a deep breath.

"To make that happen things will have to be different M."

"Different?"

"Good different."

"Different how?" I ask.

"I have no idea."

"But can't we just find a school and I go there?"

"Unfortunately I don't think so. Adam has been talking me through all the stages and forms we have to fill in again."

"But I got the diagnosis. We've got that letter."

"That was just the beginning M. If you want things to be different and I think that needs to happen, it takes time. Remember all that fighting I had to do to get your diagnosis…that letter…all the appointments? It took years."

Anxiety is near.

"Can't we stay here Mum and I could go to Sky's school?"

"In Cornwall?"

"Yes, Jackie would let us live here."

"Are you being serious M?"

"Yes! This is a world of good Mum!"

"Have you forgotten about Toby?"

"No." And I think about how much I don't like Toby but I miss him too.

"I have… He's been busy 'getting on' and I have to go back and work out how to get Toby to stay in more."

"He likes going out."

"Not really. He just prefers it to staying in."

"What school will I go to?"

"I don't know M, and I don't know how we are going to get you there but I will."

My mouth is dry. Anxiety is circling me.

I tap my face and I want to shout at Anxiety, tell it to GO and LEAVE ME ALONE! But the more I want to shout, the more it rips at my throat and pummels my body and I freeze with fear! Terrified at what it will do to me next! This controlling, unpredictable force stopping me from getting my words out, communicating and being me. Controlling me! Anxiety wants to make me angry because anger and stress and shouting feed it and make it BIGGER and nastier and crueller.

And I'm just a Year 8 from Sevenoaks and I have to face and battle and tame this Beast every day, and the only way I've worked out how is to try, really try to be in control of me and not shout and scream and rage at it and to take a…

Deep breath.

"And I know me saying 'I don't know' will make you feel anxious," continues Mum.

And breathe out.

"Not as anxious as going back to that school Mum."

Deep breath in.

"You might have to be home schooled for a few months… I don't know…"

"What's that?"

"It means still doing school work but at home."

"Who will teach me?" Mum looks into the fire.

"I'll have to talk to your dad about things and Grandma…maybe she can help out and I could talk to Steve about reducing my hours at work…or maybe get a loan for a tutor…re-mortgage the house. I just don't know exactly M, but we really do have to step into the unknown…so that we can get life right for you, and I'll do whatever it takes."

Unknown

And The Beast of Anxiety continues to creep around me. Ever present. Always waiting for its opportunity to attack. Always.

Deep breath in.

And out.

Deep breath in.

And out.

Anxiety, its terrorising glare still on me, backs away, a little.

And I know I need to step into the unknown for life to be better. I don't want a life of riding round on buses to avoid school.

I want a proper chance at life. I really think I could be good at school. I really believe that.

"Proud of you M," and she holds up the 9-Point Plan.

"I know I'm a bit different Mum."

"You are magnificent M," she says and wraps her blanket around me. Tightly.

"I love you Mum."

"I love you M."

★ ★ ★

Bella pulls on her lead as we walk along the country road towards Zennor Cove. The best place in the universe. Mum is packing the car, for our trip back to Sevenoaks.

I don't want to go back...

...but I realise I have to go back.

Bella and I tread carefully as we make our way down the narrow, rocky cliff path to the beach. I am careful not to slip in my red wellingtons.

And at the end of the path is the empty, vast beach that reaches out to the Atlantic and America and the Caribbean and the world!!!

The big, wide, scary, wonderful world!!!

I skip and run out to the shore and I look out into the horizon. The cold wind blows in my face. Hard. My eyes water, but I LOVE that nature does what it needs to do.

Volcanoes explode! Monsoons blow! The Earth shakes!

Nature – not always popular, but it doesn't change for us.

The winds rage, the sea gets angry, the sun burns, the sand shifts!

And I'm part of this world too and no one can change me either. I can't change me. God knows I've tried.

I am Nature. Being who I am meant to be.

UNAPOLOGETIC

I take a very deep breath.

I am Me.